STORM WARNING

By Elizabeth Raum

Reycraft Books
55 Fifth Avenue
New York, NY 10003

Reycraftbooks.com

Reycraft Books is a trade imprint and trademark of Newmark Learning, LLC.

Text © 2021 Elizabeth Raum

All rights reserved. No portion of this book may be reproduced, stored in a retrieval system, or transmitted in any form or by any means, electronic, mechanical, photocopying, recording, or otherwise, without written permission from the publisher. For information regarding permission, please contact info@reycraftbooks.com.

Educators and Librarians: Our books may be purchased in bulk for promotional, educational, or business use. Please contact sales@reycraftbooks.com.

This is a work of fiction. Names, characters, places, dialogue, and incidents described either are the product of the author's imagination or are used fictitiously. Any resemblance to actual persons, living or dead, is entirely coincidental.

Sale of this book without a front cover or jacket may be unauthorized. If this book is coverless, it may have been reported to the publisher as "unsold or destroyed" and may have deprived the author and publisher of payment.

Library of Congress Control Number: 2021902285

ISBN: 978-1-4788-7058-6

Printed in Dongguan, China. 8557/0421/17800

10 9 8 7 6 5 4 3 2 1

First Edition Paperback published by Reycraft Books 2021

Reycraft Books and Newmark Learning, LLC, support diversity and the First Amendment, and celebrate the right to read.

For all the volunteers, young and old, who help their neighbors during natural disasters. —ER

CHAPTERS

1. Meltdown 1
2. Current Events 9
3. Saving Ada 16
4. A Mountain of Sandbags 21
5. Jail 26
6. A Second Chance 32
7. North 37
8. Wild Rose 43
9. Saving Halloween 52
10. Grandma Lily 57
11. The Phone Call 61
12. Leaving Home 67
13. Thin Ice 71
14. Missing 78
15. Search 85
16. Teamwork 90

17. One, Two, Three	96
18. Memories	104
19. The Radio	108
20. Noah	112
21. The National Guard	118
22. Brainstorm	122
23. The Trip Home	126
24. Frozen Out	130
25. Surprises	136
26. Fireworks	143
27. Confession	149
28. Rescue	156
29. Reunion	160
30. Tomorrow	165
31. A Hero's Tale	170
32. After	174

1

Meltdown

In the fields surrounding the houses, the snow was waist deep. In some places, even deeper. Sure, some had melted, but there was still a lot to go. John Wheeler, our TV weatherman, said the winter of 1996–1997 was "one for the record books." The snow fell continuously, and it piled against whatever it hit. My friend Tyler Nelson helped me make a snow stairway up to the garage roof. We spent hours sliding down the other side into the field behind the house. It was the best sledding ever. Snow wasn't a problem … unless it melted all at once.

On April 1, Dad drove into the yard just as the school bus dropped Rosie and me at the mailbox. "North," he yelled. "Drop your books inside and give me a hand."

I tossed my backpack into the kitchen and raced back outside. Dad had already begun unloading a giant pile of sandbags from his pickup. "We'll pile them between the houses and the road. Just in case."

I groaned. "You really think the water could come up this high?"

"I do," he said. "We may be far from the river, but with so much snow in the field, we're likely to get overland flooding. If water fills the road, there's a chance it will seep into the basements. At least this will keep water out of the main floors."

I was helping Dad unload sandbags when Rosie bounded out of the house.

"I want to help, too," she said.

"Yah, right," I snorted, and then wished I hadn't because if Dad heard … But apparently he hadn't.

He smiled at Rosie. "That's my girl." He pointed to one of the sandbags we'd stacked on the snowy ground. "Go ahead. Lift it."

Rosie's the smallest eight-year-old kid in the entire second grade. She bent down, wrapped her arms around the white bag of sand, and tried to lift it. Nothing happened.

She took a deep breath and tried again. "It's stuck," she said.

I grabbed the bag, lifted it over my head, and spun in a circle.

"Show-off," Rosie said. "You unstuck it. That's not fair."

"But it wasn't—

"Now don't you worry about it," Dad said, patting Rosie's shoulder. "Those bags weigh about half as much as you do. Leave the heavy lifting to your brother and me."

"Then I'll sing for you," she said. "Singing makes the work go faster."

Dad and I unloaded the sandbags. Rosie pranced around us singing "Ring Around the Rosie." She thought she was being clever, and Dad thought so, too. This was ridiculous. I mean, next year she'll be a third grader, but sometimes she acts more like she's in kindergarten, especially around Dad. But I knew better than to say that out loud. So I tried to zone it out. Eventually, she got cold and went inside. We could finally work in peace.

We began piling the sandbags between the houses and the road. Dad stripped off his heavy jacket and rolled up his sleeves. The long, jagged scar on his left arm shimmered in the setting sun and flowed like a twisting river up his left hand to his shoulder. "A war injury," Mom told me.

One day last fall, I asked Dad, "What happened?" I figured a kid's got a right to know stuff about his own dad. Right?

Apparently not. Dad walked away without a word. But that didn't stop me wondering. He was a hero. I was sure of it.

"Stop daydreaming, North, and get to work," Dad said, and I did.

The driveway, soggy with melting snow, squished when we lifted our boots. Suddenly, Dad stopped work. He stared into the bushes near the driveway.

"What's that?" He pointed to a small pile of sticks by the side of the driveway, and then he bent down and pulled out a flat board littered with broken bits and pieces.

I had no idea what it was.

His voice got real quiet. "Look at this," he said. "Look closely."

I stared at the board, struggling to read its barely legible label: "Fair Winds Farm." I pulled back, looked up at Dad, and felt my voice go all quivery. "It's the model of the farm where you grew up."

He hurled the broken bits across the snowy yard. "It was the model of the farm."

"Maybe we can fix it?" I said.

"Forget it. The damage is done." He wanted to say more, I could tell, but Dad's not a cursing kind of guy, and this was a cursing kind of situation.

My chest got tight. I closed my eyes and tried to swallow, but it was like all those broken bits got stuck in my throat.

Dad's scowl said more than words.

I gulped and whispered, "I didn't leave it outside. Honest."

Dad either didn't hear or pretended not to. "When I gave you that model, I told you what it meant to me. I told you that your grandfather made it for my dad, and my dad gave it to me when I turned twelve. When I passed it along to you on your twelfth birthday, I asked for a promise. Remember?"

I nodded.

"And what was that promise?"

It was hard to focus on what Dad was saying. I kept asking myself how the farmhouse got outside. I kept it on the top shelf of my bedroom closet so it would be safe, and no one knew it was there but me. No one.

"I asked you a question! You promised to take care of it. Is this how my son keeps his promises?"

"But Dad. I didn't bring it out—"

"Don't lie. Don't even try. Don't make it worse." He stormed into the house. When the door slammed, I could feel it in my bones.

The model was all he had left of the farm in Wildrose, North Dakota. His parents died in a traffic accident right after Dad and Mom got married. There were lots of debts—it wasn't a good time to be a small farmer—and then I was born. They might have been able to save the farm if I had been healthy. As it was, they sold the land, the equipment, and the house just to pay the hospital bills. "This model is all I have left," Dad said when he gave it to me. "That and a few photos. The bank took the rest. I'm trusting you to pass it on to your son."

And now it was gone, and there was nothing I could do to make it up to him.

I unloaded the rest of the sandbags by myself, staggering under the weight, but I didn't stop until I had piled them into two neat rows across the front lawns just like Dad wanted.

I was almost done when I heard familiar accordion music. Whenever Grandma Lily opens her windows or the kitchen door, her music escapes. This time it was Lawrence Welk, her favorite. She loves the guy, has all his records. "He's a musician for the ages," she says.

Maybe for some ages. Not for mine. But I love Grandma Lily, and if that means listening to Lawrence Welk and his big band, so be it.

She stood at the kitchen door wearing one of the many winter caps and shawls she knitted that winter.

"North!"

I rushed over, and she handed me a small package wrapped in aluminum foil.

"Thanks." I ripped off my mittens, unwrapped the cookie, and stuffed it into my mouth. It was chocolate chip. Just out of the oven. Still melty.

"You earned it," she said and slipped into her house before I even finished chewing.

I put a few leftover sandbags around the basement window wells before I headed home. Mom, Dad, and Rosie were already eating supper.

"Dad? I finished it up."

He didn't say a word, didn't even look at me.

Rosie went over and gave him a hug. "You can have my dinner roll, Daddy," she said.

"You're a sweetheart." He ruffled her hair.

I stared at my plate and shoved a forkful of food into my mouth. Mom's a good cook, but that night it went down like sand—Gritty. Lumpy. Tasteless. Swallowing it was more difficult than lifting bags full of it.

Dad retreated to his workshop. Rosie disappeared the way she always does when it's time to do the dishes. I cleared off the table while mom turned on the hot water. We waited for it to get hot. "He's upset, North. Give him time," she said.

I was upset, too. Didn't anyone care about my hurt? It's not easy being the son of a hero.

2

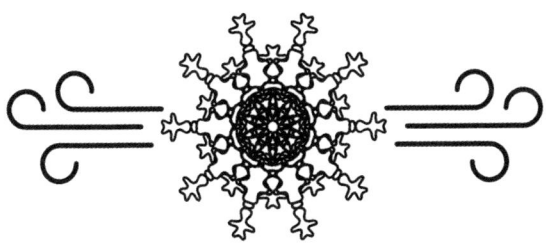

Current Events

I don't remember when I dozed off, but suddenly, I felt heavy. I could see Dad piling sandbags. Wait. He was piling them on top of me! Rosie sat on my chest yelling, "More, more!" So, he kept piling them, and Rosie kept rising higher and higher.

I jumped out of bed, looked around … I was still in my room.

Dad was gone.

So was Rosie.

And there wasn't a single sandbag in sight.

I sighed. It was only a nightmare, but it seemed so real.

I didn't dare fall back to sleep. What if I fell back into the nightmare? I opened my latest book and started reading. Just when I was finally dozing off, Rosie pounded on my door. "Get up, lazy bones. It's time for school."

"Knock it off!" I would have pretended to be sick, but Mom's too smart for that. I crawled out from under my tangled blankets, dressed, and sucked down a bowl of oatmeal. I made it to the bus with only seconds to spare. I didn't remember my homework assignment until the bus pulled away.

Wednesday is current events day in Mr. Seibert's social studies class. I was supposed to check the newspaper before bed, but after finding the ruined model, I'd forgotten about the homework. Uuf da! Mr. Seibert can sniff out undone assignments the way a cat sniffs out a mouse. He stood at the door inhaling as if he was in a donut shop instead of a classroom. I dashed past and collapsed into my desk.

Mr. Seibert strode to the front of the room. "Today is April 2, 1997," he said. "What's happening?"

Darla Klimek raised her hand. Darla specializes in weird news. The previous week she'd brought in an article about an alien abduction in Canada. According to Darla, the aliens were taking dogs from deserted highways in Alberta because "their home planet doesn't have any pets."

Mr. Seibert was not pleased. "Alien abductions are not events of national interest. In fact, they're not even real." He had said it before, but that didn't stop Darla from finding the oddest news stories. After class I told her that she spends too much time reading those creepy newspapers at the grocery store checkout line. She just smiled and said, "You should try it."

"Serious news only," Mr. Seibert warned.

"Oh, this is serious," Darla said, before reporting on a woman in Alabama who lifted a car off her husband. Darla didn't say how the car ended up on the husband in the first place, which seemed like a crucial detail to leave out. Did the wife drive over him or what? But Darla focused on how the woman used only one hand to lift the car up and save his life. "It must be true," Darla said. "It was in the *Minneapolis Star Tribune*."

It was the perfect opening for Mr. Seibert. I couldn't help but smile and silently thank Darla. Not only can Mr. Seibert detect undone assignments, but he also gets easily sidetracked.

He spent the next ten minutes talking about whether or not everything printed in the newspaper is true. Then he went on to explain that adrenaline had given the woman the strength to lift the car. "It's the body's response to an emergency situation. Adrenaline provides an energy surge that allows people to do the impossible, like lift a car with one hand. It gives us strength to do things we can't normally do. Adrenaline is nature's way of helping us in emergencies."

He would have gone on for another forty minutes if the loudspeaker hadn't crackled. "May I have your attention for a brief announcement?"

It was Mr. Christianson, our principal.

"School will be dismissed early today so that all students can help with the sandbagging down at the Wild Rice River. The Army Corps of Engineers reports that we have to add 2 to 3 feet to the dikes. All students will report to the sandbag line, health permitting."

I perked up, fully awake, and looked over at Tyler. He flexed his muscles and winked. Clearly, he was ready to build dikes. So was I. We all began talking until Mr. Seibert thumped his desk.

"School is not over for another twenty minutes. Let's return to current events."

Everyone groaned. Then Mr. Seibert looked directly at me.

"North," he said.

"Me?"

"You're the only North in this class. What current event did you bring today?"

"Um."

"'Um' is not the answer I'm looking for, but since you kids are about to participate in a current event, I'll let you off the hook this time—but this time only."

Saved by disaster.

Mr. Seibert spent the rest of the class reviewing the events occurring in the Red River Valley. "I know this isn't news, but let's have a quick review. How many blizzards this year?"

"Seven," Darla shouted.

"How much snow?"

"One hundred ten inches." Darla again.

"Which is causing?" Mr. Seibert asked.

"Floods!" we all shouted at once.

"Precisely. The melting snow has no place to go, so it turns farm fields into giant lakes. Add the ice melting in the rivers, and we have the ingredients for a major flood. Think about what happens when the ice in the Red River starts to melt."

Darla's hand was up and waving even before Mr. Seibert finished asking the question. I suspect that my sister Rosie is the Darla of Second Grade.

"Yes, Darla? Do you have a question?" Mr. Seibert asked.

"A comment," she said. "I thought rivers empty into the ocean."

Tyler snickered, but Mr. Seibert hushed him.

"They do, or at least they empty into other rivers that eventually reach the ocean. But the Red has a long journey before that. What's unique about the Red River?"

"It twists?" Darla asked.

"Yes. And flows ... " He waited for an answer. He didn't get one.

"North?" he said.

I shrugged. "Um ..."

"It flows ... North?" he asked again.

"North!" Darla shouted. "The Red River flows north."

"Yes," Mr. Seibert said, and everyone laughed. My face got hot and tingly, and it probably flashed brighter than Rudolf's nose, so I bent down to look for something—a pencil?—under my desk. When I finally looked up, Mr. Seibert was drawing an S-shaped line on the board. It reminded me of Dad's scar.

"This is the Red," he said. "When the snow melts, it fills the Wild Rice River and the Marsh Creek, and when those rivers are full, they flow into the Red. The

Red can only hold so much. When the Red is full, it overflows its banks and floods other rivers, as well as the land and towns along the way."

"Oh, I get it," Darla said. "If the Red floods, so will the Wild Rice."

"That's right," Mr. Seibert said. "And our little town of Ada, Minnesota?"

"Is headed for disaster," Darla said.

And that's why we were getting out of school early. With luck, we'd save the town. I'd do my part. In fact, I'd do more than my part, lots more. The flood was giving me a chance to start over, a chance to prove to Dad that I wasn't a loser after all.

3

Saving Ada

We all cheered when the bell rang. Sure, the flood was serious business, but it was fun, too. A National Guard unit was in town working on the dike. Tyler and I joined a group made up of Cougar football players. Tyler's older brother Donny is a wide receiver on the team. Donny's fast. So is Ty. When we get to high school, he'll be a wide receiver, and I'll be the quarterback. Tyler and I practiced all fall. We didn't stop until the thermometer hit zero and the snow kept tripping us up.

"You guys stand next to Coach," Donny said.

"Really?" Ty asked.

"Sure. He'll be your coach one of these days." He hit Ty on the shoulder. I have to admit, I was jealous. It would be cool to have a big brother instead of a pesky little sister.

Donny and several other football players stood on a flatbed truck loaded with sandbags. They lifted the bags off the truck to the guys on the ground, who passed them to Coach Norland.

Coach passed them to Ty.

Ty passed them to me, and I handed them off to Buzzy Ogard, an eighth grader. Buzzy's brother is a running back. I don't know who took them next, but they must have ended up on the riverbank.

"How much do these things weigh?" Ty asked.

"About 35 pounds," Coach said. Coach taught math. "Here's a real-life problem for you kids. We've already emptied an entire flatbed. The engineers told me there are 22 pallets per truck, and each pallet holds about 100 sandbags. So, how many pounds of sand are we lifting?"

I got tired just thinking about it. I tried to do the math in my head. Tyler beat me to it."

"Let's see," he said. "Twenty-two pallets of 100 sandbags equals 2,200 bags. That's easy."

"Right," Coach said. "Now at 35 pounds each."

Ty took his time. We passed another five or six sandbags before he blurted out, "77,000 pounds!"

"Exactly," Coach said.

No wonder I was getting tired!

When it got too dark to see, the National Guard hooked up powerful lights. "Spotlights," one of the boys said.

"Floodlights," Coach said, and everyone laughed. I felt like I was already part of the team.

We worked till ten that night. Ty and his brother dropped me off at home.

Mom told me Dad was still down at the river. I hadn't seen him. He must have been working with a different crew.

I staggered to my room and stripped off my wet socks and pants. It was as if I'd been standing in a shallow lake all night. My arms were duck bumpy. I jumped into the shower and cranked the water to sizzling. When I got out, my arms dragged behind the rest of my body. When I hit the bed, they fell asleep before my legs did.

School let out early again on Thursday. The crowd at the dike was even larger. People from other towns—towns further from the river—joined in to help. There were college students, too, from Moorhead State University in Moorhead, Minnesota, fifty minutes southwest, and a church group from Fergus Falls, an hour and a half southeast of us. Every single person worked hard. Kids Rosie's age passed out bottles of water. Grandmas poured hot coffee out of thermoses, and the Red Cross handed out peanut butter and jelly sandwiches.

One of the engineers directed Tyler and me to join another sandbag line. I counted as I lifted sandbags. I lost count at 247 bags. Ty stopped long before that.

My neck was sore. So was my back. Lifting the heavy sandbags was taking a toll on everyone. There was less joking around. People didn't laugh as much. But we still worked hard.

Around ten o'clock, Dad found me working the line with Tyler. "Time to call it quits for the night," he said leading me back to his pickup.

I glanced over at him as he drove home. Dad looked beat. "Long day?" I asked.

"Yah. It's been a long winter. If we can just get past this flood, we'll be fine."

"The flood and the baby," I said.

Dad reached over and ran a hand through my hair. "That's right. The flood and the baby." He was quiet for a few seconds, and then he said. "North, I saw you working with your friends. You did well." It was the nicest thing Dad had said all winter.

I couldn't stop grinning. Lucky for me, the pickup's cab was dark.

When we got home, I skipped up the stairs.

4

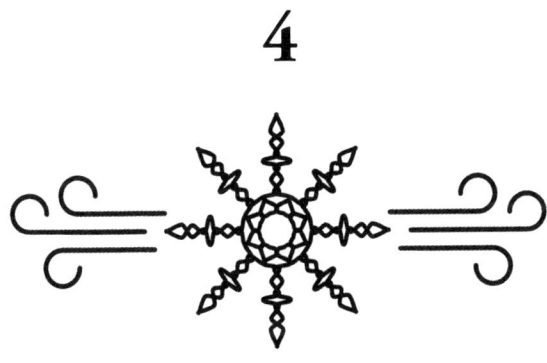

A Mountain of Sandbags

At breakfast Friday morning, Mom said, "They're predicting 10 inches of snow this weekend."

"No more!" Rosie moaned. "I want spring."

"We all do," Dad said. "But don't worry. Spring follows winter as surely as Monday follows Sunday. It's just taking its time this year."

Then he turned to Mom. "River's high enough as it is. If we get more snow, we'll need to raise the dike even higher. I'll go straight to the river after work. I may even leave early if I can manage it. You and Rosie have supper on your own. North and I will grab a sandwich later."

There was no question that school would let out early again on Friday. "It's been a great year," Tyler said. "First we had all those snow days and now this."

"I'm afraid you'll pay for those days off," Mr. Seibert said. "The school board may extend the school year."

Everyone groaned.

"Just be thankful you have a school to go to," he said.

Thankful? We all groaned again. Well, everyone except Darla. She loves school.

Me? Not so much. I mean school's okay, but I'd rather play football or video games. If English was a video game, I'd ace it. I actually do pretty well in math and science, and I love woodworking class. When I told Grandma Lily that I was thinking of becoming a carpenter, she said, "You do that. Woodworking is a wonderful skill. Imagine building something so beautiful that it brings joy to everyone who sees it."

The bell rang just after lunch. We raced to the river.

"We're trying to reach a total height of 903 feet above sea level," the crew supervisor said. "The river level is rising, and with snow in the forecast, we can't take any chances. This battle is not over yet."

The snow along the riverbank had turned to mush. The soggy ground grabbed onto my boots and made rude sucking sounds with every step I took.

Around suppertime a light rain began falling.

A church van circled the area, giving out cheese sandwiches and cups of steaming coffee. Normally, I'm not allowed to drink coffee, but that night I took one. The coffee tasted bitter, but the warmth felt good. I inhaled a sandwich and gulped more coffee. Then it was back to work.

After another hour of hauling sandbags, one of the men told us to hold up. "The engineers are taking measurements." It felt strange to be standing still.

"They don't need us here," Tyler said. "Let's take a hike. I haven't seen the dike up close."

"Me neither." We walked along the riverbank to a section of dike that was finished. It was about 6 feet tall and extremely wide. I wasn't surprised because Coach said the base of a dike has to be three times the height.

"Remind you of anything?" Tyler asked.

"A big pile of snow."

"Exactly. A mountain of snow," Tyler said, and then he yelled, "Race you to the top."

I should have stopped right there.

I should have said something wise, like "That's not a good idea, Tyler."

But I didn't.

Maybe it was because I was tired after lifting all those sandbags.

Maybe it was because I'm the kind of kid who screws things up.

Whatever. I never said a word.

Tyler scrambled up the dike, and I was right behind him.

Tyler moved fast. He knocked a couple of sandbags loose. They skidded toward me.

I jumped aside and that sent another one sliding. It hit the ground with a thud.

Tyler reached the top of the dike first. "I won!" he yelled. "That makes me king of the hill."

At that exact moment, one of the giant spotlights flashed on. It caught Ty in its beam, his arms outreached, a triumphant grin on his face.

"Get off the dike!" a voice boomed. "Now!"

Ty's face turned whiter than the snowy sandbags. He lowered his head and began picking his way toward me. When he got close, he whispered, "Don't turn around."

Which is exactly what I did. There were hundreds, maybe thousands, of people staring up at us. They were shaking their heads and whispering to one another. They were people I knew—kids from school, family friends, neighbors. And each and every one of them was mad at Tyler and me. We were as much the enemy as the river.

I scanned the crowd, hoping, praying, that Dad wasn't there. Just this once, Lord, let him be late. But there he was standing near the back, his hat in his hands, his shoulders slumped. If he glared at the river the way he was glaring at me, it would have snuck back into its banks and flowed quietly away. I had to force my feet to move forward.

5

Jail

Two National Guardsmen were waiting at the bottom: one with a megaphone, the other controlling the light. By the time I reached them, the crowd had gone back to work.

"The engineers are coming," one guardsman yelled to the other. "They'll check for damage. We may have to rebuild this entire section. We don't know the extent of the damage, but at least a few sandbags were displaced."

Rebuild? It had taken hours of work to build it the first time. My hands began to shake. I shoved them into my pockets.

I wanted to sink into the soggy ground and disappear.

I wanted to be a little kid again and home in bed.

I wanted a do-over.

I didn't look up until the guardsman began talking.

"Don't you boys know enough to stay off the dike? What were you thinking? Tampering with a dike is against the law."

Tyler's dad stepped up and put his hand on Ty's shoulder. "They weren't thinking," he said. "They're just kids. It was a mistake, for sure, but it won't happen again, will it?"

"No, sir," Ty said.

"Absolutely not," I mumbled. "We didn't mean …"

My dad stood next to the officer. He spoke so softly that I had to strain to hear. "You said it's a crime, isn't it? Tampering with a dike? Maybe the boys should spend the night in jail."

Jail? I couldn't believe it. Sure, I'd done something wrong, but it wasn't as if I'd killed somebody or stolen a million bucks. Pastor Johnson is always talking about forgiveness. We're supposed to forgive one another. Why couldn't Dad forgive me?

Instead, he scowled at me. Before he could say anything else, Tyler's Dad jumped in. "No need for that," he said. "It would be better to put them back to work. Make them pay for their crime with hard labor."

The officer nodded.

Tyler and his dad walked back toward the sandbag line. His dad's arm cradled Tyler's shoulders.

"Sir?" the guardsman said, turning to my father.

Dad looked at me. "Dumbest thing you've ever done," he said. "I don't know if I trust you down here." Then he turned to the guardsman. "I'll take the boy home. It won't happen again."

It was the longest two miles I'd ever traveled. I perched on the edge of my seat, as close to the door and as far from Dad as possible.

At first, Dad didn't say a word. We were halfway home when he finally spoke.

"I don't know what you were thinking. And don't tell me it was Tyler's idea. If he told you to jump off a bridge, would you do it? If he told you to skip school? Or steal candy from the country store? Would you do that? What were you thinking? Oh, you weren't thinking were you? First the farmhouse, and NOW THIS. HAVEN'T I TAUGHT YOU ANYTHING?"

I didn't say a word.

I couldn't.

Words stuck in my throat.

I didn't move a muscle.

Didn't even blink.

I was afraid if I opened my mouth, I'd bawl like a baby.

Dad stared at the road ahead. I stared out the side window. My own guilty face stared back at me. I shut my eyes.

Was it just last night that I'd sat in Dad's truck feeling proud of myself? For once I'd done something good. It sure hadn't taken me long to mess up again.

Dad pulled into the yard and signaled for me to get out. "Tell your mother I'll be late," he said, and took off down the road.

I stood for a while in the cold drizzle watching the headlights fade into the mist. If I stayed outside, I'd probably catch pneumonia and die. I imagined Dad standing over my coffin at Grace Lutheran. "I should have treated the boy better," he'd say, a tear sliding down his cheek. "But at least we've got Rosie and the baby." Mom stood nearby holding the new baby while Rosie sang and danced around the coffin. Everyone clapped.

Wait just a minute!

Who was I kidding?

They probably wouldn't even miss me. Why should I give them the satisfaction of getting rid of me so easily? Nope. No drizzly death for me.

I stepped inside. I stripped off my jacket, boots, and socks by the back door. Even my underwear was wet, but I wasn't about to take it off downstairs.

Mom and Rosie laughed at something on TV. I smelled popcorn.

I snuck past and up to my room. If I stopped to give her Dad's message, she'd want to know why he brought me home early, and I couldn't bare to see Mom's eyes when she heard what I'd done.

Dog followed me and curled up on the rug beside my bed. "Good boy," I said rubbing him under the chin. "You still love me?" He looked up at me with smiling eyes and drooled all over my hand. I took that as a yes.

Dog slept with me that night. He snores, but that's not what kept me tossing and turning. I kept seeing Dad's face—the way it looked at the dike. The memory was worse than any nightmare. Could I ever make it up to him?

The next morning, I popped up early and dressed in my work clothes. Maybe—if I was ready to go—I could convince Dad that I wanted to repair the damage

I caused. I caught him in the kitchen. "Please let me go. I want to help. I'm sorry, Dad. I'm really sorry."

"You had your chance."

"Come on. Give me a break. I know it was wrong, but I just wasn't thinking."

"You've got that right. You weren't thinking. That's why you can stay home this morning and practice thinking more clearly." He started out the door, and then he turned back. For a second or two, I thought he might change his mind and let me come along. Instead he told me to help Mom. "She's worried about the baby. It's due any day."

"Is something wrong?" I asked. Every time she went to the doctor, she came home with glowing reports.

"No. No, I didn't mean that. It's just that … well, give her a hand if you can. And if she needs me, if anything happens, call 911. Tell them I'm at the dike and it's an emergency."

I suppose, in a way, he was giving me another chance. I was in charge of Mom. I'd rather have been down at the dike, no question about it, but Dad hadn't discounted me completely. Seconds after he left, Rosie pranced by singing, "North's in trouble. North's in trouble." I almost said, "Knock it off." But I clamped my mouth shut, and that, at least, was something Dad would have approved.

6

A Second Chance

Mom had seemed distracted lately. Over the course of the winter, she grew gigantic. If she kept growing at this rate, we'd have to make the doorways wider. Luckily, the baby was due to pop out any day. I kept thinking about the movie *Alien*, where the creature claws its way out of an astronaut's body. Sure, I knew that Mom's baby wouldn't do that, but even so, it all seemed a bit creepy.

Mom came up with a long list of chores. That's her style of punishment. It works. I swept, dusted, and vacuumed. Finally, she told me to wash the kitchen floor. It was pretty muddy.

"No mop today," she said. "The only way to get this floor clean is on your hands and knees."

I spent an hour on my knees surrounded by suds. Rosie burst into the kitchen when I was almost done. "Rosie!" I yelled. "You messed up my floor," but she wasn't listening. She flicked on the radio. "More storm warnings."

"... and rain will turn to snow," the announcer said. We listened to a report that the Wild Rice River was "rising quickly with water flowing over both Highway 9 and Highway 200."

Mom waddled in, sank into one of the kitchen chairs, and rubbed her belly with both hands. "Oh!" she said, but she wasn't listening to the radio.

"What's wrong?" Rosie said, at the exact same moment I said, "Is it the baby?"

Mom nodded. She hunched over and gripped the table's edge. I grabbed the kitchen phone.

"Not yet, North. Give me a minute."

Rosie and I froze in place.

Mom finally straightened up and said, "There. I'm fine. It was just a twinge."

"Dad said to call."

"Not now, North. He said he'd be home for lunch at noon."

I glanced at the kitchen clock. It was 11:50.

"Better dump that dirty water, North. Rosie, let's you and me go upstairs. I have some last-minute packing to do."

"Packing?" Rosie asked. "Is it time?"

I didn't hear what Mom said, but Rosie's whoop echoed off the walls.

It only took me a minute to rinse out the mop bucket and put it away. By the time Dad drove into the yard fifteen minutes later, the floor was dry. He stormed inside dripping dirty slush all over my clean floor.

"How's your mother?" he asked.

"She had a twinge."

"Why didn't you call me?"

"She said—" but before I could finish, he was pounding up the stairs calling Mom's name.

"I'm fine," she said as they came back down. "Stop fussing, Robert. North and Rosie didn't exactly rush into the world. I don't know why this little one should be any different. But perhaps we should think about getting to the hospital. In this weather and with flooded roads, it will take us more than an hour to get to Fargo, and there are storm warnings again."

Mom sat down at the kitchen table while Dad called Grandma Lily. "She's fine," he said, "but we want to beat the storm. You sure you can handle the kids?"

It wasn't that we needed a babysitter. Having Grandma Lily next door meant Mom and Dad wouldn't have to worry about us. If any problems came up, Grandma Lily would be there. She'd been there as long as we could remember. She's Mom's grandma, and that makes her our great-grandmother, but she's the only grandmother we've ever known.

"Are you sure Lily is up to the challenge?" Dad asked as soon as he hung up.

"Of course she is," Mom said. "She'd be hurt if we insisted the kids come to the hospital, especially in this weather. Besides, North's old enough to keep an eye on Rosie."

Rosie puffed herself up and stamped her feet. "I'm old enough to keep an eye on myself. I don't need North telling me what to do."

Dad patted her on the head. "But I feel better knowing that you have a big brother who can deal with emergencies—not that you'll have any."

There it was again—it was like Dad was giving me a gift. He said he trusted me even though I'd made mistakes—lots of them.

Rosie stuck out her tongue and stomped off.

"I shouldn't be gone all that long," Dad said, "and I'll check in by phone. If I'm not home by bedtime,

I'll be here by the time you wake up in the morning. If you need anything, call Lily. Your mother and I are depending on you. No screwups. Promise me that you'll take good care of your sister."

"I promise."

At the time, it didn't seem like such a big deal. I knew what Dad meant. No fighting. No bickering. It wouldn't be easy—not with Rosie—but I'd do my best. I'd make Dad proud. After all, I'd made a promise, and Dad always told me that promises are sacred.

Dad helped Mom into her warm winter coat. She insisted on giving us hugs before she headed to the car. "We'll call you when the baby is born." Mom lingered in the doorway. "And stay inside. There are storm warnings again. Hard to believe it's April 5. Next time I come home, I'll be holding your new brother or sister in my arms."

"Sister! Be sure it's a sister!" Rosie shouted.

Dad held an old umbrella over Mom's head. The mix of snow and rain was already blanketing the car.

"I'll be home soon," Dad said. It sounded like a promise. Then he slipped into the car and drove away.

7

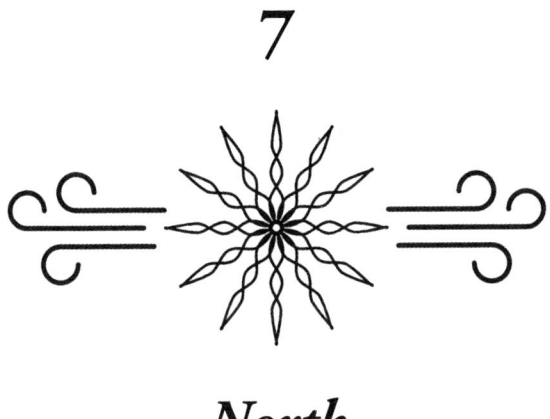

North

Rosie and I stood at the kitchen window watching the car's taillights blink out of sight. "I'm going to watch TV," Rosie said. She danced out of the room as if she was on stage. Rosie plans to be an actress. One show at the community theater, and she's convinced that she's ready for Broadway.

I was still standing at the window when the phone rang.

"How you kids doing?" Grandma Lily asked. I could hear music in the background. This time it was country, probably Gene Autry, another of her favorites.

"We're fine."

"It's no problem for me to come over," she said.

Even though Grandma Lily lives right next door, she's

too old to go outside in stormy weather. Not that she thinks she's old. "I'm just creaky," she said one day. "I just need to oil these joints, and I'm as good as new."

"You can do that?" Rosie asked, which made Grandma Lily collapse on the sofa laughing. "Ah, Precious, if only it worked like that."

"North? You there?" she asked when I didn't respond right away.

"I'm here, and you don't need to come over. We're doing just fine," I said again.

"Well, you call me if you need anything, North. You hear me?"

"Yes, ma'am."

I wandered into the living room. Rosie was in one of her television trances. Her eyes bugged out, mouth open, head tilted toward the TV.

"I'll be in my room," I told her. "Call me if you need me."

Adrenaline had carried me through the last few days. Exhaustion hit all at once. I was asleep in seconds.

"North! North! Wake up!"

Rosie pounded my shoulder. "Ow! What's the big deal, anyway? Can't a guy get some sleep?"

"It's Dog," Rosie said. "I can't find Dog."

"What time is it?"

"Three o'clock in the afternoon. Did you think it was the middle of the night?"

I did. But I didn't tell Rosie that. "Where's Dog?"

"If I knew, I wouldn't have woken you up," Rosie said.

I stretched the sleep out before I started down the stairs. "Dog! Come here, fella!" I called.

Dog was nowhere in sight.

"Dog! Here, boy."

No Dog.

Sometimes Dog wanders down to the basement, and although that seemed unlikely, I opened the cellar door a crack. "Dog!"

"I could have told you he isn't here," Rosie said. "I already checked."

I opened the kitchen door, the one that leads outside, and pushed aside the storm door. "Dog!"

An icy blast hit me in the face. The wind roared. But Dog didn't.

"He must have gone outside." I took a minute to slip into my winter jacket. It was still damp. I had stuffed a mitten into each pocket. They were wet, but they would have to do. I pulled on my boots.

Before stepping outside, I told Rosie to stay put. "Don't come out."

"Don't worry. I'm not going out there," Rosie said. She closed the door behind me. I heard the click as the dead bolt locked.

"Rosie! This isn't funny. I could die out here."

Rosie opened the door. "Oops. I didn't mean to lock you out." She smiled sweetly. I couldn't tell whether or not she was joking.

Sleet slapped my face. The rain was turning to snow. The gray day didn't provide much light either. I should have brought a flashlight. "Dog!"

Puddles filled the yard. Water overflowed the road. It was only an inch or two deep but enough to fill the ditches. I couldn't see Dog anywhere. I scanned the horizon. On sunny days I could see for miles across the flat farm fields, but not that day. Sleet got in the way. I peered into the dogless gray mist.

There was no sign of Dog at the front of the house.

I hoped Dog would be waiting to come inside at the side door into the kitchen. But he wasn't. He hadn't run away. He couldn't. Dog lumbered. There was no run left in him.

I scanned the yard. Water lapped against the bottom of the garage door. I walked over to check it out and that's when I heard a whimper.

"Is that you, Dog?"

The whining grew louder.

"I'll have you out in a minute, boy."

I reached into the water and lifted the heavy overhead door. Dog stepped outside and rubbed his cold fur against my leg. "Let's get you inside, old boy," I said, pulling down the garage door and heading for the kitchen.

Dog limped up the steps to the kitchen. He ambled to the center of the kitchen floor and shook. And then he lay down with his back tight against the stove.

"Yuck," Rosie said. "He smells like a wet dog."

"He *is* a wet dog."

"Where was he hiding?" she asked.

"I don't think he was hiding. He must have gone into the garage for shelter when we let him out earlier. Then, when Mom and Dad left, he didn't get out in time. He was trapped in there. He's been wet and cold for a few hours now."

I grabbed one of Mom's fluffiest towels from the downstairs bathroom and rubbed him down. He rolled onto his back, looked up at me, and smiled his best Dog smile. If Dog was a cat, he would have purred. As it was, the second I stopped rubbing him, he nudged my hand with his nose, so I rubbed him some more.

He settled down with his back against the stove. He sighed and fell sound asleep. I felt cozy lying next to him. Wet dog smells much better than any old perfume.

Dog's comfortable—not only to lie on, but to be with. He never expects anything of me. Dog's not like Dad. Whatever I do is just fine with Dog. I gave him a pat on the head. "You're a lazy dog," I said, but he knew I didn't mean it—not really. Dog is 100 percent mutt. He's got nothing to prove.

We've been together a long, long time. Dog is a year older than me. When they first brought the puppy home, Mom and Dad gave him a dog name: Rover. It wasn't original, but it worked. At least it worked until I was born. I couldn't say Rover, so I called him Dog. Soon everyone did. Mom and Dad forgot his real name until the day they found an old photo of baby me sitting on Dog's back, horsy-style. Dad held me tight. On the back Mom had written, "Heigh-Ho, Rover."

I framed that picture.

8

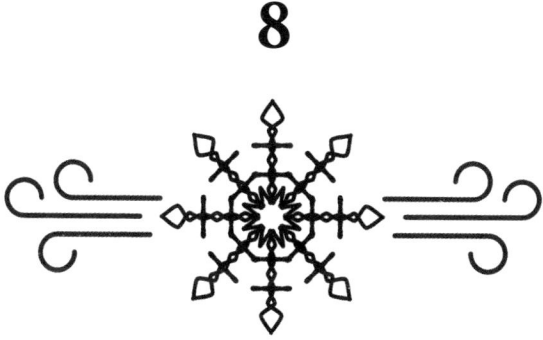

Wild Rose

Rosie snuggled up next to us, ignoring the wet dog smell. "I'm getting worried. Do you think Mom's had the baby yet?"

"Dad will call," I said. "He promised."

They'd been gone for about four hours. It wasn't raining anymore, but when I looked out the kitchen window, I saw water flowing from the fields into the street and creeping over the land toward us. If it kept coming, we'd be in trouble. Our houses—Grandma Lily's and ours—sit at the top of a small slope. I suppose the land looks flat to someone from a mountainy place, but in Ada we sit high, at least higher than the road.

"Watcha looking at?" Rosie asked. "Is it Daddy?" she asked. "Do you see his car?"

"Nope. It's too early."

"I'm hungry," Rosie said.

My stomach grumbled agreement.

I ran downstairs and grabbed one of Mom's casseroles from the fridge. It had a white label with the words *Beef Noodle* on the top of the aluminum foil. Mom made tons of hot dishes for when she was in the hospital and first home with the new baby. "We'll appreciate having supper ready," she had said. I knew she wouldn't mind us digging in ahead of time.

We finished eating, and I was clearing away the dishes when Rosie popped back into the kitchen.

"I just watched John Wheeler's weather report," she said. "He says this is turning into another blizzard. That will make eight this year, North. Maybe we won't have school Monday!"

"Of course, we'll have school. Today's only Saturday. They'll have all day tomorrow to clear the roads. Besides, it's already April. We won't get much snow this late in the year."

"We might," she said. "I don't want to miss any more days. What if they won't let me into third grade next year."

"Oh, they will. I'm sure of it."

Rosie sighed. "That's good." I followed her into the living room to catch the sports.

"When's Dad gonna call?" Rosie asked.

"When the baby's born."

"How long does it take for a baby to be born?"

"I don't know."

"How long did I take?" she asked. "You were there, weren't you?"

"Not exactly. I was home with Grandma Lily. Besides, I was only five years old."

"But now you're twelve. Guess how long it takes."

"Forty-nine hours," I said.

"It can't take that long. How long does it really take?" Rosie asked.

"I have no idea. We have to wait and see."

"Oh." Rosie was obviously disappointed in me, and then her face suddenly brightened. "Did I tell you they're going to name the baby Annie?" she asked.

"What if it's a boy. This family needs another boy."

"No. No. No. It has to be a girl, a girl named Annie."

"Well, if it is a girl, they'd never name her Annie."

"They will," Rosie said as she flounced out of the room. "I already asked."

They certainly hadn't chosen normal names like Annie for either of us. My real name is North Dakota Olson, and Rosie's is Wild Rose Olson. We're named after the town and state where my father grew up: Wildrose, North Dakota. When I asked Dad why he and Mom had given us such weird names, he said that with a last name like Olson, a person needs a distinctive first name.

"Olson's not all that common," I told him.

"Really? How many Olson families in Ada?"

"In Ada? Five, maybe, counting us."

Dad handed me the local phone book.

"Sixteen," I said.

He tossed me the Fargo/Moorhead phone book.

I riffled through the pages until I came to Olson. Olsons covered three pages. Each included five columns of densely packed Olsons.

"See? Now look for my name."

I counted fifteen Robert Olsons.

"And how many North Olsons?" he asked.

There wasn't a single one.

"And you won't find a Wild Rose Olson there either. When you're surrounded by Norskis, you have to work at being different."

I dropped the phone book on the table and sagged against the fridge.

Dad smiled like he wanted me to appreciate his cleverness. But he didn't have to live with the name —well, not the way I did. I'd have been happy to be another Robert Olson, although now I knew that living up to my dad's idea of what it meant to be a man was hard enough without also having to live up to his name.

Whatever they named the new baby, I was pretty sure it wouldn't be Annie.

Rosie popped back into the living room wearing her red *Annie* wig and carrying her *Annie* video. "Ta-dah," she said. She shoved the video into the VCR. "Watch with me, North."

"No way. I've seen *Annie* a gazillion times already. Besides, I've got work to do."

Rosie pouted, but her snit didn't last long. Even before I left the room, she was bouncing on the couch, singing the *Annie* songs.

While I was washing the dishes, Tyler called. He said his Dad was still sandbagging. "The water's coming up fast, it's snowing, and the wind's blowing at 60 miles an hour. It's a blizzard out there. Mom wouldn't let me go. She said it's too cold. You know how she is."

I did. Tyler's Mom grew up in Florida, and everything about winter in the Northern Plains scared her. Whenever I met Ty at his house last winter, his mom would wrap a scarf around his face before she'd let him go outside. Then she'd kiss him on the nose and say something momish like, "You've got such a cute little nose. I don't want you to freeze it off. Don't catch frostbite."

"I won't," Ty said, and we'd run outside before we started laughing. After all, frostbite isn't something to catch like a baseball or a cold. Besides, we were smart enough to come inside before our faces froze.

"She's worried about Dad, too, but he's a grown-up. Wish I was," Tyler said. He took a deep breath before rushing on. "Anyway, Dad says everything will be fine if we finish the dike."

"John Wheeler says we're getting more snow. Maybe if everything freezes, the flooding will stop," I said.

"Maybe for now, but eventually it's all gonna melt. There's a lot of water still running free. We've got water in the basement already. We moved everything upstairs."

"Your basement flooded? I'd better check ours," I said, and hung up.

As soon as I turned on the light, I saw water. There were still a few dry spots, especially near the stairs, but puddles dotted the cement floor.

I couldn't tell where the water was coming from. Every spring we have some seepage around the window wells. Water drips down the concrete walls. But this was worse. The whole basement was flooding.

What would happen to the washer and dryer, the furnace, and the water heater? And what about all the stuff stored there? Mom stored cartons of Christmas decorations in one section and canned foods in another. Grandma Lily's preserves and her spaghetti sauces filled more shelves. My old tricycle parked in the basement along with family pictures Dad brought from the farm in Wildrose. Mom's box of letters, the ones Dad sent from Kuwait, sat on one shelf next to boxes of summer clothes and picnic things ready for summer.

Dad stored the fireworks in a box in the basement, too. Every year on July 5, Dad and I drove across the North Dakota border to Starr Fireworks and bought a supply for the next year. Big signs promised that we could Buy One Get Two Free, so we stocked up.

I couldn't do much about the furnace or the washer and dryer, but at least I could save Dad's model airplane collection, the photos, Mom's letters, and the fireworks.

But I'd need Rosie's help.

"Rosie!" I called.

She didn't answer.

She probably heard me over the *Annie* video. I knew she was singing along with the orphans. She knew the show by heart. She had played the role of Molly in the community theater production. Everyone said she was terrific, but they didn't have to sit though all six performances like I did.

She glanced over at me. "Next time we do the play, I'll be Annie," she said.

"Sure, you do that," I said. "But right now we've got problems, and I need your help."

"I'll help later. Can't you see I'm in the middle of something? If these floors aren't perfect, Miss Hannigan will tan our hides."

"Stop pretending, Rosie. This is worse than Miss Hannigan. The basement's flooding. We need to move stuff upstairs." I actually growled. My hands formed fists. I felt like punching something, and that something was Rosie. But I promised Dad I'd take care of her, and punching her wouldn't help get the job done.

I took a deep breath.

In.

Out.

In.

Out.

My hands fell to my sides, and I felt calmer. "What if we turn up the volume so you can still listen to *Annie*?" Then another idea smacked me in the head. "If we don't work fast, all the Halloween costumes will be lost in the flood."

She snapped her head toward me. "What did you say? The costumes will be lost?"

Rosie loves Halloween, not because she loves candy—even though she does—and not because she loves scary things—which she doesn't—but because she loves costumes. Rosie and her friends play dress-up all year long.

"I need those costumes," Rosie said. "I asked Mom to let me keep them in my room, but she said no. But now I'm gonna move them upstairs so they'll be safe." She cranked up the volume on the VCR and followed me to the kitchen. "Let's save Halloween!"

9

Saving Halloween

I put on my boots and made Rosie slip into hers before we headed down the basement stairs. We sloshed through rapidly rising water. It covered the toes of my boots and was creeping toward the laces.

I handed Rosie a box of letters. "Here. Take this."

"This isn't costumes."

"You're right," I said. "But I can't get to the costumes without moving some other stuff." That wasn't actually true, but it worked. Rosie took the box.

"Where do I put it?"

"Upstairs. Anywhere."

"The kitchen?"

"Sure."

Rosie lugged the box up the stairs.

I shivered and stamped my frozen feet, wishing I'd worn boot socks and made Rosie wear them, too. It was too late now. We didn't have much time left. Water trickled through the window wells. The puddles on the floor kept growing.

We used empty laundry baskets to haul the canned food and Dad's models upstairs. I carried up the heavy box of family photos and went back for another box of letters. They were already damp. I hoped they weren't ruined.

Rosie took most of the Halloween stuff. She worked hard, and she didn't give up. She sang as she worked: "I Think I'm Gonna Like It Here," "Little Girls," "Maybe."

When the music ended, Rosie stopped so quickly that I bumped into her. "You little pig dropping!" she said to me. "You do like *Annie*. You can't deny it. I heard you singing along. You sang *Annie* songs!"

"Not me," I said even though she was right. I'd vowed never to sing those songs, but I'd been singing along without missing a word. I didn't even know I'd been doing it. I might not catch frostbite, but I'd caught *Annie*.

"Ooh, little girls!" I said, taking on Miss Hannigan's role. I hated to admit it, but I know the script by heart, too.

"You don't scare me," Rosie said.

I chased her up the stairs. "Get to work," I said.

"Nobody loves me!" Rosie yelled.

"Get to work, and I mean now!"

Rosie collapsed in laughter. We marched back down the stairs and started hauling up the final loads singing "It's the Hard Knock Life."

I carried the heavy box of fireworks upstairs. We had only a couple of loads to go when the lights flashed. They didn't come back on.

"Oh!" we both cried at once.

I couldn't see a thing. Not even Rosie.

"North, what happened? I'm scared."

"It's okay," I said. "Wait here, and I'll get a flashlight."

"I'm NOT staying here by myself," Rosie said.

"I'm right here," I said. "Talk so I can find you."

When she spoke, her voice was no more than a whisper.

"Let's sing," I said. I began singing "It's the Hard Knock Life." It was a good choice, I guess, because Rosie joined right in, her voice getting stronger and stronger.

I followed her voice until our hands collided. I gripped her hand in mine and led her toward where I figured the stairs would be.

"Ow!" I yelled.

"What happened?"

"I stubbed my toe on your old tricycle."

"Carry it up for me. Please," Rosie said.

"No way. We'll leave it here. You're too big for it anyway. Just step over it."

"But North. What if our little sister needs it?"

Sister? But I didn't bust her about that. "It will have to wait till the lights come on. I'll get it later."

"Okay," Rosie said, letting me pull her up the stairs and into the kitchen.

The whiteness of the snow falling outside the window made things a bit brighter. I found the flashlight that Mom keeps in the silverware drawer. We yanked off our boots and plunked down on the kitchen chairs.

The lights flashed back on.

"Oh!" Rosie cried. "I was getting worried."

Me, too. But I didn't say it. I promised Dad that I'd take care of things at home. So far, I'd saved at least some of the stuff in the basement. That was quite enough, thank you. It was time for Dad to come home.

10

Grandma Lily

"I'll be watching television," Rosie said.

"Fine." I didn't have the energy to worry about Rosie watching too much TV, but I had begun worrying about Grandma Lily. I couldn't sit still. I felt fidgety. Was she all right? Did she have electricity? Should I go over and check on her?

Grandma Lily's lights shimmered through the foggy window. Usually, just looking at her house gives me a warm-from-the-oven-chocolate-chip-cookie kind of feeling. But I couldn't see her moving around inside her house. That didn't surprise me. She spends her evenings in the living room knitting and listening to her big old-fashioned radio or her phonograph.

She picked up on the first ring. When I heard Peggy Lee singing in the background, I took a deep breath and relaxed. I could picture Grandma Lily in her cozy red robe knitting in time to the music.

It isn't only Grandma Lily who loves Peggy Lee. Rosie does, too. I remember when Grandma Lily told Rosie that Peggy Lee was a small-town girl who became famous. "She was born in Jamestown, North Dakota, and her real name was Norma Deloris Egstrom."

"I'm a small-town girl who will become famous," Rosie said, and started trying out new names: Rosie Lee Olson. Peggy Rose Lee. Rosamund Wilder. As if her name, Wild Rose Olson, weren't weird enough.

"Let me turn down the record player," Grandma Lily said when she picked up the phone. "Are you kids okay?"

"The electricity—"

"It was probably ice on the wires or that blustery wind. Would you children like me to come over there for the night? It'll only take me a minute to pack a bag."

"No need," I said. "We're fine."

"Well, then, I suggest you get to bed early. Wrap up in your quilts. If the weather report is right, it could get mighty cold tonight. I don't want you freezing your toes off." Grandma Lily laughed her raspy kind of laugh. "I think I'll turn in, but call me if you need anything."

Now that the electricity was back on, our house was cozy warm. I lingered in the kitchen. It was a mess. Boxes were scattered everywhere, but at least we'd saved what we could. I reached into the box that held Mom's letters. I grabbed a handful, still in their envelopes. As I pulled the folded pages from one envelope, ink ran down the edges. I laid the wet wad onto a towel and tried to pat it dry. The others were even wetter. Even the box was damaged. They were letters Dad sent to Mom when he was in Kuwait with the Minnesota National Guard. Mom saved them all. He saved hers, too. I could see a few of my drawings sticking out of the envelopes. I remember drawing him a picture every day he was away. Now they were a runny, soggy mess.

The box of photos was in better shape. Only a few on top were wet, so I laid them out on a dish towel to dry. Deeper in the box, I found Rosie's baby pictures. The first ones showed her in the hospital in an incubator. Rosie considers herself a miracle. "I had to fight to survive," she brags. "Nobody thought I'd make it."

That's when I remind her that farmers put baby chickens in incubators, too. And then I start clucking.

I don't remember much about those days, except that Mom and Dad were gone all the time. I stayed with Grandma Lily. We played with squirt guns, I remember that, and we filled balloons with water and threw them at each other. We did puzzles, too. Mine had sixteen pieces; hers had more than a thousand, and when I knocked the pieces onto the floor, she didn't scold me. We laughed and picked them up together. When Rosie finally came home, I kept going back to Grandma Lily's. She always had time for me, even when no one else did.

Deep down in the box, beneath Rosie, I found photos of me. There was one of me taking my first steps, me in a stroller at the mall, and at the very bottom, Mom holding me when I came home from the hospital. She's smiling down at me as if I was a miracle, too. Maybe I was, at least for a while. By the time Rosie came along, I was strong, healthy, and not very new or interesting. Lucky for me, I had Grandma Lily.

Looking at little Rosie and little me reminded me of the new baby. Why hadn't Dad called? Was there a problem?

And that's precisely when the phone rang.

11

The Phone Call

"Dad!" I yelled.

Rosie popped into the kitchen so fast that I jumped, which made her laugh.

"Let me talk to him," she begged.

"No way." I lifted the receiver high above Rosie's head.

She tried to snatch it, but she couldn't reach high enough.

"What's going on there?" Dad said. "Are you kids all right?"

"We're fine," I said, putting the phone back against my ear.

"You're Mom's doing well, but it's going to be a while."

"You don't need to worry about us."

"Are you and your sister getting along?"

I glanced over at Rosie, who sat on a kitchen chair pouting.

"No problems here," I said fingers crossed. It wasn't exactly a lie. We weren't actually fighting. At least, not yet.

"Well, then, if you kids are doing all right, I think I'll stay a while longer."

"Yah. Mom needs you."

"She does. I was with her when you and Rosie were born …"

"And you'd like to be there for this new kid, right?"

"That's right," Dad said, and it sounded like he was smiling.

"Like I said, we're fine." And we were. The electricity had returned, and even though the basement had flooded, there was nothing Dad could have done about it.

"Thanks, North. It means a lot to your Mom. I'll call back in an hour or so. Now let me talk to your sister."

I signaled Rosie and handed her the phone.

"About time," she said to me, and to Dad, "Is she born yet? When? How long does it take?"

I scooted closer to hear Dad's answers, but Rosie shoved me away.

"Okay, I love you," she said and hung up the phone.

"So, what did he say?" I asked.

"Wouldn't you like to know?"

"Yah, I would." But Rosie simply smiled at me as if she had solid information to withhold. Well, if that's the way she was going to be, I had something to hold back, too.

"Guess I'll have a dish of ice cream," I said making it pretty clear that I wasn't going to get any for Rosie.

"North!" she yelled. "Okay. I'll tell you. He said she's not born yet; it might take a few more hours, but he doesn't know for sure. So, can I have some ice cream, too?"

I opened the freezer door at the exact moment that the lights flashed off. Then they flashed back on. The clock on the microwave oven blinked 12:00, 12:00, 12:00. I reset it.

"What's happening?" Rosie whispered.

"It's just the storm."

I dug around in Mom's emergency drawer until I found a candle and some matches. I wanted them nearby in case the lights went out again.

"Take off that ridiculous wig and get into your pajamas, and then we'll have ice cream." I used my best imitation of Dad's voice, which actually sounded a lot like his until my voice cracked.

"You're not in charge of me!" Rosie said. She sneered at me and ran her fingers through the scraggly red curls before she marched off to her room to put on her bunny pajamas. She kept the wig on in silent protest. "So, how about that ice cream?"

I dished out several big scoops. Cherry vanilla for me. Chocolate for Rosie.

When we finished, Rosie carried the empty dishes to the sink. "Now can we play a game?"

We sat at the kitchen table and played Crazy Eights, but I couldn't concentrate. The wind whipped against the house, and cold drafts seeped through invisible cracks in the wall. It was as if we were under siege from enemy artillery.

I wished Dad would call or, better yet, drive into the yard. Even with all the lights on and the television blabbing in the background, the house seemed empty. It needed Mom and Dad as much as we did. It had been over two hours since Dad called. He'd promised to call back. Why hadn't he?

"I'm going to bed," I said after about the fifth game. "You can keep the flashlight, I've got the candle and some matches."

"Dad said no candles in our rooms, North."

"Well, Dad wasn't talking about emergencies. Besides, I'll only light it if the electricity goes off again." I held the candle in front of me as I climbed the stairs to my room.

"I'm waiting for Dad," Rosie said.

"Whatever." I snuggled under the covers fully dressed. My body sank into the mattress, but my mind refused to relax. Questions piled up like the winter's snow—

Had the baby been born?

Was Mom okay?

Was the baby healthy?

Why hadn't they called? Maybe the phones were out in Fargo.

Should we have gone over to Grandma Lily's?

Rosie didn't wait up long. I heard her clomp up the stairs to her room.

And then she began to sing an old tune from Sunday school. She sang all the verses and then started again:

> *All things bright and beautiful,*
> *All creatures great and small,*
> *All things wise and wonderful:*
> *The Lord God made them all.*

She really does have a pretty voice, sweet and sure. It's a lot like Mom's. I stopped twitching and settled deep into the mattress. I'm not sure whether Rosie stopped singing before I fell asleep or not, but it felt nice either way.

12

Leaving Home

I woke up shivering. I reached over to turn on the light by my bed, but nothing happened. The house was dead quiet and freezing cold.

As I fumbled around in the dark for the candle, my lamp crashed onto the floor. My fingers finally hit wax and the box of matches beside it. I struck a match, lit the candle, and slipped out of bed. I pulled the quilt around me like a cape and tiptoed down the hall.

Mom and Dad's bed was untouched.

The living room was empty, and the kitchen was dark and quiet except for the soft sound of Dog's snoring. He'd fallen asleep while we played Crazy Eights and hadn't moved an inch since.

"Morning, Dog."

He stretched and ambled to the door.

It's too cold for that, I thought, but Dog didn't have a choice. I led him to the kitchen and opened the door. Dog stepped out into the cold, dark world. I closed the door quickly and tried flicking the kitchen light switch. Nothing happened.

No lights.

No heat.

No stove.

No television.

No Dad.

I picked up the phone to call Grandma Lily, but the phone was dead, too.

Add Grandma Lily to the "no" list.

I heard Dog whining and let him back in. He shook icy sleet onto the kitchen floor.

I wandered into the living room. The battery clock on the wall ticked softly. It was seven in the morning, but the sky was midnight dark and sleet pounded against the windows. I wished we had a fireplace like Grandma Lily. Maybe when Rosie got up, we'd go over there. We'd sit around the fire and roast marshmallows. We could boil water for hot chocolate. Those thoughts warmed me until I checked the thermostat on the wall. The needle pointed to 50 degrees above zero. It felt like 50 below. I pulled the quilt tighter.

I wandered back into the living room and sat in Dad's favorite chair. I tried to read his *North Dakota Horizons* magazine, but every article seemed to be about record-breaking temperatures or the Children's Blizzard of 1888. I tossed the magazine aside. I nodded off, but as soon as my head dipped forward, I jerked awake. What was it Mr. Seibert said during our winter weather unit? Something like "extreme cold puts people to sleep, and they never wake up."

Rosie! What if she was dead in her bed?

I raced up the stairs, balancing the candle in one hand and holding the quilt around me with the other. I dashed into her room. She was completely hidden beneath a pile of blankets. When I pulled them back to check her, she bolted upright. "North, get out of here." Then she pulled the blankets back over her and scooted beneath them. Problem solved: she was alive.

I shook my head and walked to the door but turned back when I heard her muffled voice. "Are Mommy and Daddy home? Is the baby born yet? I'm cold. Can you turn on the heat, North? Please?"

"I been thinking that we should go over to Grandma Lily's. She's got a fireplace."

"Could we roast marshmallows?" she asked.

We may not have much in common, but we both love roasted marshmallows.

I held the candle while Rosie put socks, sweatpants, and a sweatshirt on over her bunny pajamas. She followed me to my room while I added a few layers. "We better bring the flashlight and candles just in case," I said.

"In case of what?" Rosie asked.

"In case Grandma Lily runs out," I mumbled. "I'm not sure what else to bring."

"Dog," Rosie said. "And my *Annie* video and my *Annie* doll and my *Annie* pillow." They're special. Remember? The director gave them to everyone in the cast."

Fine … if that made her happy. A cold and hungry Rosie is bad enough without adding a mad Rosie.

13

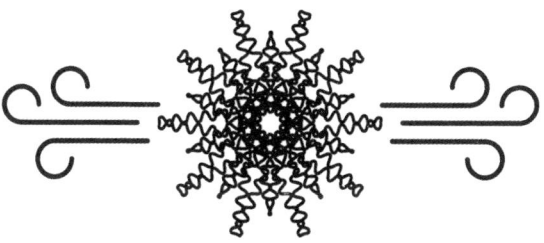

Thin Ice

"Hurry up," I snapped. Why did it take Rosie so long to pull on her boots? I wanted to see Grandma Lily. I had a strange feeling that something wasn't right, but I'd been wrong before. I shrugged it off.

Grandma Lily is the most independent person I know. She may be old, but she's got lots of energy. Last summer she climbed up on a ladder and painted the trim on her windows. "That's too much at your age, Lily," Dad said, but she shushed him. "At my age, I'll do as I please. And today, I wanted to paint my windows. They won't need it again for five years." She winked at me and whispered, "Who's going to tell a ninety-one-year-old what she can or cannot do?"

Not me, that was for sure, and not Dad either. It was like Mom always said, "Grandma Lily will outlive us all. She certainly outworks us!"

But when I glanced at her house on that cold morning, something didn't look right. I shivered, and it wasn't just the cold. Maybe Rosie's worry had leaked onto me.

Our kitchen door opens to the same side of the house as Grandma Lily's. All we had to do was cross the driveways to reach her door. It's not far, only about 30 feet.

Rosie took her time. "I'm too cold to move fast," she said.

She put on her snow pants, buckled her boots, and wrapped a scarf around her neck. Finally, she donned her coat, hat, and mittens. She looked warm and toasty, but all those layers made walking difficult. She rocked back and forth like one of her Weeble people. I slung my knapsack over my back and grabbed the flashlight. It was still dark outside.

"Where's Dog's leash?" I asked.

"Search me," Rosie said.

I settled for the long piece of clothesline rope that Dad keeps beside the coat hooks. "Never know when a bit of rope will come in handy," he says.

I tied the rope to Dog's collar. He looked at me as if to say, "What's going on?"

"You're coming with us," I told him and opened the door to a wicked windchill.

Neither Dog nor Rosie moved.

"We'll get frostbitten," Rosie cried.

"Not if we hurry, and not if we stay dry. Let's go!" I said.

"Maybe we should wait," Rosie said. "What if Dad calls?"

I stepped back into the house, picked up the phone, and held it to Rosie's ear. "What do you hear?" I asked.

"Nothing," she said. Her voice sounded small; her eyes were wet with unshed tears.

"We have to go," I said gently. Then I sweetened the deal. "Those marshmallows are waiting."

This time, Rosie didn't hesitate. She followed me to the door and outside.

"Give me the flashlight," I said to Rosie.

I shined the light toward Grandma Lily's house. It played over the yard. Ice covered both driveways. A couple of white sandbags poked through the ice. I'd stacked a few bags of sand around the basement windows to hold any floodwater at bay.

We could barely see Grandma Lily's door through the snow. Wind howled wolflike around us. I had to pull on Dog's rope; he didn't want to leave the house. Smart dog! I didn't really want to go outside either, but something was spurring me on, which proved to be a good thing.

The kitchen steps were icy. Rosie slipped. I grabbed her before she fell down the stairs.

When I stepped off the bottom stair, the ice held. I'd been afraid I'd sink into icy water.

Rosie followed. "It's like a skating rink," she said. She pranced around playing skating star.

"Stop! You're on thin ice."

But I was too late.

Rosie stomped down hard and broke though.

"Oh! It's cold!"

When she tried to stand up, she slipped again and fell full-length into the water. She lay on her stomach. Water covered her from her shoulders to her toes.

"Help! I'm freezing."

Any other time, I might have thought she was being dramatic, but Mr. Seibert had taught us about hypothermia during one of the first blizzards. Icy water is especially dangerous because it pulls heat from the body.

I reached out to pull Rosie up, but I let go when the ice cracked beneath my feet. I dropped the flashlight, and it disappeared into the icy water. It was deeper than it looked. I moved onto safer ground.

"Try to crawl back onto the ice," I yelled over the roaring wind.

She tried. "I can't."

"You have to!"

"Please help me."

She sprawled in the icy water. Only her head and shoulders were visible.

"Give me a minute," I said. I took off my gloves and unhooked the rope from Dog's collar. I slid along the ice until I reached Grandma Lily's kitchen stoop. I looped one end of the rope around the railing and tossed the other end to Rosie.

"Grab it and move when I pull."

"Got it," Rosie said. She grabbed the rope and held tight.

I gave it a mighty tug.

"No!" she cried as the rope slithered out of her hands. One of her woolen mittens clung to the rope.

I slid over to where it lay coiled like a snake, ready to attack. I yanked the mitten loose and tossed the end of the rope to Rosie.

"My hand is too cold," she cried.

"You have to."

"I can't."

And I couldn't leave her laying in an icy puddle.

"Look, Rosie, you grab the rope, and I'll pull you out. I know you're cold now, but as soon as we get inside, I'll make you hot cocoa, and we'll toast marshmallows. Close your eyes and think of the cocoa."

Rosie closed her eyes.

"Can you see it?"

"Yesssss." She reached for the rope.

"Hold tight!"

I tugged with every ounce of strength I had on that rope, and Rosie moved forward.

I pulled again. And again. Inch by inch, ever so slowly she slid out of the icy water and onto the snow.

"I did it!" she cried. Rosie let go of the rope and pulled herself upright. She wobbled toward the steps.

"Good job!" I said, more to myself than to Rosie. My arms felt like I'd been lifting sandbags at the river.

Rosie grabbed the railing. Her lips looked blue and her legs were unsteady.

"Let's get inside." I motioned her forward. We weren't safe yet.

"Not without my *Annie* doll and my pillow." I need them. They remind me of the show."

I doubted she'd ever forget her role as Annie—or let us forget it, either.

"Where are they?" I yelled over the roaring wind.

"There." She pointed toward the icy water.

"Sorry, kid, but there's no way I'm going back there." I yanked on the kitchen door and pushed Dog and Rosie inside. It was dark and quiet except for Rosie's crying.

I wanted my flashlight, too, which I'd dropped when Rosie fell.

"Grandma Lily," I called. "Grandma Lily!"

But there was no answer, no answer at all.

14

Missing

"Maybe she's asleep," Rosie said. "I'm freezing."

"Asleep? Grandma Lily never sleeps late. I'll go check on her."

"No, North. I'm freezing. You have to help me."

Grandma Lily's house was even colder than ours. I rubbed my hands together, but it didn't make them any warmer.

"I'm too cold to move."

"If you don't move, you'll freeze in place. Your legs will get frostbite and your toes will fall off. You'll never be able to dance in *Annie* again."

Rosie whimpered. "I can't do it alone."

Her teeth chattered, and she was shivering. Of course I'd help. That's what big brothers do, and what I'd promised Dad. I ran into Grandma Lily's bathroom and grabbed five or six fluffy towels off the shelf. Then I started pulling on Rosie's boots and socks. They were frozen stiff, but I managed to yank them off. I wrestled her out of her wet outer clothes, and then attacked the sweatpants and sweatshirt. I tossed the soggy mess onto the kitchen floor. She was still wearing her fuzzy bunny pajamas.

"You can do the rest yourself," I said and pointed to the bathroom.

She left wet footprints as she dashed across the hall to the bathroom.

I opened Grandma Lily's kitchen junk drawer and found a flashlight. When I turned it on, I saw six candles lying in a row beside two boxes of kitchen matches. Grandma Lily is like that. "There should be a place for everything and everything in it's place," she says when I help her to straighten up her garage. She keeps everything in perfect order. I helped her label the shelves.

While Rosie finished drying herself off, I checked the fireplace. The firewood I'd hauled in from the garage the week before was neatly stacked beside it. It seemed odd that Grandma Lily hadn't already started a fire herself, but I didn't think she'd mind if I got it going. After all, I'd watched Dad make fires for years. I knew to open the flue, lay down the kindling, pile up a tepee of wood, and then light it. "Careful with the matches." Grandma Lily said, every time I lit the fire. So did Dad.

"Fire's started, Rosie," I called. She hobbled into the living room wearing a pair of my outgrown jeans and one of Dad's ripped T-shirts.

"Where—"

"Grandma Lily's ragbag," she said.

That made sense. Grandma Lily never threw anything away. Her ragbag was full of old clothes and bits of fabric.

"Do you like my socks?" Rosie asked. She was wearing an old pair of striped boot socks. "There's a few holes, but they work."

She settled on the couch and covered herself with Grandma Lily's favorite afghan. The fire roared to life. Dog and I sat on the floor in front of it. The warmth felt great.

"Where's Grandma Lily?" Rosie said.

Good question. She must have heard us. She's always up early. Whenever Rosie or I fuss about going to bed, Grandma Lily always says, "Early to bed, early to rise, makes a man—or in my case, a woman—healthy, wealthy, and wise."

"Grandma Lily," I called softly, as I walked down the hall to her room. "Are you awake?"

The door to her bedroom was open. I peeked inside. The bed was made, as if she'd been up for hours—or hadn't even slept in it. I checked her sewing room across the hall. She wasn't there either. I began to shiver, and it wasn't just that I'd left the cozy fire behind me.

Rosie had fallen asleep on the sofa. She popped up when I stirred the fire.

"Did you find her?" she asked.

"Not yet."

When she stood up, the afghan tumbled to the floor. She followed me down the hall wrapped in a fluffy purple towel.

"Grandma Lily!" she called in a singsong voice.

I called even louder, but there was no answer.

We rechecked every room in the house. Rosie even looked in the closets, which seemed silly, but we were out of hiding places.

"She's nowhere," Rosie said.

"She has to be somewhere." I stumbled into the dark kitchen and opened the basement door. Water reached all the way to the fourth step from the top. I shined the flashlight into the water, leaning over the stairs as far as I could without tumbling down them. The flashlight reflected off the water. There was no way she could be down there. If it was like our house, the water had seeped in slowly. If she'd been in the basement, she'd have had time to escape before it flooded. I closed the door. She had to be somewhere else. But where?

"Maybe she went into town," Rosie said.

"And just how would she do that?" Grandma Lily doesn't drive; she doesn't even own a car. And she is too sensible to walk the two miles to town in a blizzard. And even if she had, she would have stopped at our house first.

"A taxi?" Rosie suggested.

"And when was the last time you saw a taxi in Ada, Minnesota?"

"Never?"

I crossed my arms and stared at Rosie.

"It's not my fault, North." She stomped her feet.

"Sorry," I said. "It was as good a guess as any."

"Where's Dad?" she said. "Why hasn't he called?"

I plunked down on the sofa. Rosie plopped down next to me. She leaned against me the way she would have leaned against Dad. So I stood up, and Rosie tumbled onto the sofa cushions. I didn't want Rosie depending on me. I wanted Dad. We needed a real man in the house, not a screwup like me.

I watched the fire. "Firewood!" I shouted. "Maybe she went to the garage for firewood."

"But there's already a big stack," Rosie said.

"Not enough to last us very long. Not if it stays this cold and the electricity stays off."

I sat down by the fire and waited.

And waited.

And waited some more.

"How long does it take to get firewood?" Rosie asked.

"Not this long," I admitted. "I'd better go check outside." I'd check the garage first, then maybe the shed, then …

"Stay with me," Rosie said. "Don't leave me all by myself. I'm scared, North."

"I am, too, but you want me to find Grandma Lily, don't you?"

Rosie nodded.

"I won't be long," I said, hoping I was telling the truth.

15

Search

I pulled on my coat, boots, and gloves. They were so cold and wet that they didn't give much protection against the storm, but I didn't want to take time to search Grandma Lily's closets for something dryer. If she was outside, I had to find her quickly, or it would be too late. It might already be too late. I hit myself upside the head for waiting so long.

Grandma Lily's garage and ours sit next to each other like twins. Ours is the strong, healthy twin; hers is the 98-pound weakling. The inside is neat and organized, but the outside tilts and the roof leaks.

A sheet of ice stretched from Grandma Lily's house to her garage. If I stepped lightly, I could glide along the treacherous ice. I took tiny skating steps to the garage door. I couldn't risk falling, not with Rosie depending on me.

I stooped to lift the rickety old door. It wouldn't budge. I knelt down to get a better look. Ice gripped the bottom of the door, and it wasn't about to let go.

I slid over to check ours. It was frozen, too, so I worked my way down the narrow alleyway between Grandma Lily's deck and her garage to the side door. She usually keeps it unlocked but closed tight. It was slightly ajar. I gave it a push.

"Ow."

"Grandma Lily!"

I poked the flashlight through the opening and peered inside. She was lying on her side half covered in water, her body wedged against the door.

"Grandma Lily. What happened?"

She groaned in response. I pushed lightly against the door. Grandma Lily cried out again. If I pushed any harder, I'd hurt her. I took a deep breath, pulled my body tight, and squeezed through the narrow opening.

Blood dripped down her face. I lifted her red knit cap and used it to wipe away the blood oozing from a gash on her forehead. I pressed her cap against the cut, and the bleeding slowed.

"Grandma Lily?"

She opened her eyes and looked directly at me. "Slipped in the bathtub," she stammered.

Bathtub? There was no bathtub in the garage, and if she fell inside, then how did she get outdoors. It was crazy talk.

"It's cold out here," I said. "You've got to get inside. Can you get up?"

She moaned and said, "Toothpaste," which made about as much sense as the bathtub. Her whole body was shaking. I didn't know what was wrong, but I knew I had to get her inside, and do it quickly.

She was too heavy for me to carry. Or was she? I remembered that newspaper article Darla Klimek brought for current events. If a skinny woman could lift a car off her husband, then I ought to be able to lift Grandma Lily.

I bent down and wrapped my right arm around her neck. I moved my left hand closer to her knees, but when I tried to push my arm under her knees to get a grip, she cried out.

I pulled back. What if I made whatever was wrong worse? It was slippery outside. Even if I lifted her up, I might fall on the way to the house. The path was pure ice. I couldn't take a chance. I laid her head down as gently as I could and stood up.

Several logs were scattered near where she lay. Grandma Lily must have come for firewood, slipped, and been unable to get up. She knew the wood stacked by the fireplace wouldn't keep us warm for long. She knew that Rosie and I would come to her house. That's just the way she is. She knows stuff before the rest of us do.

I swung the flashlight around the garage and saw snow shovels, garden tools, and her wheelbarrow. If I could get her into the wheelbarrow, I could push her to the house. No, the thin ice wouldn't hold a wheelbarrowful of Grandma Lily even if I could lift her into it, which I doubted. I looked past the garden hoses and lawn furniture and spied the red plastic sleds that Rosie and I store in Grandma Lily's garage.

The sleds might work!

"Grandma Lily?" She stirred but didn't wake up. I called to her and jiggled her hand.

"Wha ... ?" she said groggily.

"We need to go inside. Can you lift up a bit to get onto this sled?"

"Sled? I'm tired. Don't wanna go sledding."

If I hadn't been so worried, I would have laughed. I couldn't imagine Grandma Lily whizzing down a hill on a sled like Ty and I do. "You're not going sledding. I'm taking you home."

"Warm," she mumbled. It was more crazy talk. She wasn't warm. She was close to frozen.

Grandma Lily didn't move, didn't even lift her head.

She's tall and gangly. There was no way I could gather up all her parts and slide her onto the sled. I'd already tried to lift her once and failed. There was no point in trying again.

When I joined the Boy Scouts last year, I studied first aid. If I didn't warm her up, Grandma Lily could die of shock or hypothermia right there on the floor of her garage.

"I'll be right back," I whispered in Grandma Lily's ear, and then I slipped back outside and slid all the way to the kitchen door.

16

Teamwork

"Rosie!"

No answer.

"Rosie!"

I raced inside, afraid that something terrible had happened to Rosie. But no, she had curled up on the sofa and fallen back to sleep between several colorful quilts.

"Get up!" I yelled, shaking her shoulder a bit roughly. "I need your help. It's Grandma Lily!"

"What did you do to her?" Rosie asked.

"Do to her?" I snarled. "I'm trying to save her life, but I can't do it alone. Put your coat on. You have to help me save Grandma Lily."

"Save her?" She jumped up and ran to the kitchen. I grabbed the quilts in both arms and followed.

"Hurry, North! We have to save her." She picked up her frozen parka.

"Not that one. It's too wet. Put on one of Grandma Lily's."

Rosie pulled an old flannel jacket off the hook by the back door. It fell to her knees, but it would have to do. "Find some boots and meet me in Grandma Lily's garage."

I grabbed bandages, gauze, and tape from Grandma Lily's bathroom and raced out the door. "Meet me in the garage," I yelled as I rushed past Rosie.

A few seconds later, I reached the garage. Miracle or no miracle, I hadn't tripped on the quilts or dropped the bandages.

Grandma Lily looked like one of the corpses on a cop show. I could imagine someone drawing a chalk line around her dead body. I touched her neck trying to find a pulse, but I couldn't feel a thing.

She groaned.

I jumped.

The dead do not groan. She was still alive.

Her right foot turned out and looked shorter than the left. I tried to remember exactly what that meant, but everything I learned in the Boy Scout first aid course blurred together. Whatever it meant, it wasn't something good.

I threw a quilt over Grandma Lily, ripped open a package of bandages, covered her cut, and wrapped gauze around her head. The bleeding had slowed to a dribble. When I finally found the pulse in her wrist, it seemed weak and as fluttery as a moth trying to escape through a screen.

"What's wrong with her?"

I jumped.

"Rosie! Don't sneak up on my like that."

Rosie dropped to her knees beside Grandma Lily and began asking her questions. "What happened? Did you fall? Are you okay? What should we do to help?"

Grandma Lily didn't say a word. She didn't even open her eyes.

"She must have come out to get firewood and fallen," I told Rosie. "Her head's cut, and something's wrong with her leg. We have to get her inside. If we don't, she may die."

"Don't say that!"

"It's the truth. We have to get her inside, and we can't waste time."

"Did you forget 911?" Rosie asked in her know-it-all voice.

"Did you forget the phones aren't working?"

Rosie whimpered.

"Stop sniveling and give me a hand." I felt bad as soon as I said it. She's just a little kid. But I've seen those tears before. They're not real. They're actress tears —"North's being mean" tears. Tattletale tears.

I handed Rosie the second quilt and pushed some patience into my voice. "Try to ease this beneath her. But be careful. There's something wrong with her leg ... or her hip. I think she broke her hip."

That was it. Mr. Jensen, our Scout leader, told us about the time his mom broke her hip, and how he knew exactly what to do. The story made it easier to remember.

1) He laid her down—Grandma Lily was already lying down.

2) He covered her with a blanket—check, I'd done that.

3) And then he called 911, which I couldn't do.

4) But then he told us that while he was waiting for the ambulance, he gently bound her legs together with wide straps.

Wide straps? I spotted the pile of old sheets that she uses to cover her tomatoes on frosty nights. They would do. I cut a wide strip off one of them and tied her legs together as gently as I could. Finally, I had a plan.

"Why are you tying her up?" Rosie asked.

"So we can move her without hurting her. You keep working on the quilt." It wasn't completely under Grandma Lily yet. We needed it to help us lift her. "I have to make a stretcher."

I grabbed Grandma Lily's Magic Scizzors. They'd arrived in the mail a few months ago. "These scissors will cut anything," she said when she opened the package and handed it to me. I read it out loud:

"Powerful Magic Scizzors cut anything and everything—crack nuts, crush garlic, cut through hardened steel!"

Rosie had grabbed the package. "But they spelled scissors wrong."

"Let's hope that's the only thing they got wrong," Grandma Lily said. She put the scissors on the shelf in her garage and used them to cut her rose bushes, wire, and the plastic border around her garden. They had no trouble cutting through the plastic sleds, either. I cut one end off of each one, and then I duct-taped them together. Finally, I placed the taped-together sleds alongside Grandma Lily. They were long enough! Now all we had to do was lift her over the lip onto the sled and hope that the tape would hold.

17

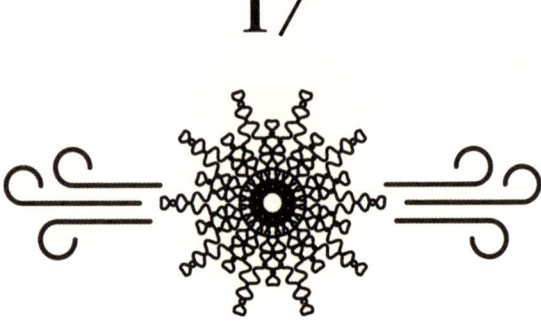

One, Two, Three

Rosie needed help getting the quilt under Grandma Lily. The quilt seemed to stick to the wet floor, which made it even harder.

"I'll push her up while you pull the quilt under her," I said.

Push.

Pull.

Push.

Pull.

We finally managed to get the soggy quilt beneath most of Grandma Lily. "Now we have to lift her," I said.

"Not much. Just enough to get her into the sled."

Rosie stood up.

So did I.

"She's so big," Rosie said.

"But she's not heavy," I said. "All that dancing kept her skinny."

That made Rosie smile. Grandma Lily looked silly when she danced.

"You take her head. I'll take her bottom half," I said.

"Get a firm grip," I said, "and on the count of three, lift."

One.

Two.

Three.

Up and over.

"We did it!" Rosie yelled.

We hadn't lifted her more than two inches high, but it was enough. "Now let's get her inside."

The makeshift stretcher coasted the short distance to the house. Rosie skated ahead and held the kitchen door open while I carefully lifted the front of the sled, where her feet were, onto the bottom step. There were two more above it.

"Stop!"

"What … ?"

"Look, North! She's sliding off."

Rosie was right! Grandma Lily was slipping backward off the sled. I pulled the sled back onto even ground as fast as I could without bumping it on the ground.

"Maybe you should turn it around so her head goes up first," Rosie said.

I didn't see how that would help. Feetfirst or headfirst, she'd still slip off the sled.

"We could tie her in," Rosie said.

"We'd have to tie her head to foot, and that won't work. Give me a minute." I studied the situation. The stairs were steep. If Dad was home, we could carry her up, holding the sled even, but Dad wasn't home, and Rosie couldn't lift one sandbag, so how could she lift an adult? There had to be a better way.

"Come back out and stand by her for a minute," I said.

Rosie clomped back down the stairs. "Where are you going?" she cried as I raced off.

"To check things out!" I ran to the front of the house. No one ever uses that door. I tried to open it.

It was locked. But there was only one step, and it was a small one.

I ran back to Rosie. "Go inside and unlock the front door. We can take her in that way."

I didn't have to repeat the order. Rosie dashed up the stairs so fast I was afraid that she'd slip. A few minutes later, she was back.

"I don't know how."

"Then stay here," I said. "I'll do it."

I raced inside, through the kitchen, and into the living room. The door was unlocked. I tried to open it. No luck. It was stuck. I pulled again. And again. And finally, it burst wide open. I didn't bother to close it.

When I got back to Rosie, I told her to go back inside. "Meet me at the front door."

Then I pulled the sled to the front of the house. It was easy to push the sled up the one short step. "We did it!" I said.

Rosie clapped. "Wow!" she said. "We did it! We got her inside!"

I pulled the sled into the living room and collapsed on the sofa. I sat back, arms out, wanting nothing more than to stay there forever. But we weren't done.

"Now, we've got to warm her up." I shifted the sled in front of the fire, and then I ran to the bedroom, pulled blankets and pillows off Grandma Lily's bed, and hauled them to the living room.

"We have to take her wet clothes off," Rosie said.

She was right, but I couldn't do it.

"You're a ... woman," I said. "You'll have to do it. And be careful of her right leg. I think she may have broken something."

For once, Rosie understood. "I'll try."

While she was busy, I ran to the kitchen and picked up the phone, and dialed 911. The phones were still dead.

When I got back to the living room, Rosie pounced on me. "I did it all by myself!" She'd yanked, ripped, and pulled the wet clothes off Grandma Lily. And then she'd covered her with blankets. She even pulled the wet quilt out from beneath.

"Good job, kid."

I added another log or two to the fire. When I turned around, Rosie was smiling. I was pretty sure it was because of what I said. I never guessed that something I said could mean much of anything to Rosie. I'd have to think about that, but first I had to check Grandma Lily. She seemed to be sleeping peacefully. I couldn't think of anything else to do for her.

Dog stretched, and then he wandered over to investigate the new arrival. I sat staring at the fire, watching the embers flare and fade,

flare and fade,

flare and fade ...

I must have dozed off, because I was startled when Rosie said, "It's a great fire, North."

"Thanks, Rosie." Maybe she was growing up. I couldn't remember when she had ever admitted that I'd done something right.

She fussed over Grandma Lily. "Do you like the fire?" she asked as she knelt beside Grandma Lily's still form. Rosie pulled at the blankets to free Grandma Lily's hands and rubbed them. She patted Grandma Lily's cheeks and murmured words of comfort. Grandma Lily slowly opened her eyes and smiled.

"She's awake!" Rosie yelled.

But before I could get there, Grandma Lily had closed her eyes again.

"What's wrong with her, North? We should call the doctor."

We should have, of course, but how? I opened the drapes and looked outside. In the dim morning light, I could see ice and water, water and ice, and more snow beginning to fall. The road was gone, hidden beneath floodwater and chunks of ice. We were completely cut off.

Rosie wandered into the kitchen and poured herself some cereal. She carried it into the living room and settled close to the fire. "Cozy," she said.

"Scoot back," I yelled. "You don't want to burn that Annie wig right off your head, do you?" She scowled at me but moved away from the fire.

"I'll bet church is canceled," Rosie said. "Let's check the radio."

"Can't," I reminded her. "No electricity."

Rosie just smiled and took off down the hall to Grandma Lily's sewing room. She came back a few minutes later with an old battery radio. "You forgot about Grandma Lily's emergency radio," she said triumphantly as she fooled around with the dials.

"—and in Ada, according to reports from callers, rising water from the Wild Rice River and the Marsh Creek have caused massive flooding. Outlying areas are struggling with overland flooding. Electricity is out, and these folks are trying to keep warm in the midst of one of the winter's worst blizzards."

"That's us," Rosie yelled. "They're talking about Ada."

"Shh. I'm trying to listen."

The announcer continued. "As far as we can tell, things are going from bad to worse in Ada. Hang in there, folks. This is Jack Sunday and Sandy Buttweiler, ready to take your calls at radio station KFGO, the Mighty 790 on your radio dial. We're here for you."

"They're here for us," Rosie said. "What does that mean?"

I had no idea. All I knew was that things were bad enough already and Jack Sunday said they were going to get worse.

18

Memories

It was spooky seeing Grandma Lily so still. She's always moving. She dances around the kitchen, sometimes with Rosie, often by herself. She usually has a polka or a waltz playing in the background. A while ago she took up country line dancing at the senior center. That's when she became a big Garth Brooks fan. She even considered learning to play guitar. She would have, too, if the arthritis in her hands hadn't started acting up. "Best stick to my dancing," she said, and she had no trouble convincing Rosie to be her partner.

They entered the Senior Citizen Talent Competition in February and won first prize in the Oldster-Youngster category. Rosie made a big deal of it, even though the only other contestants in their category demonstrated birdcalling ... badly. Old Mrs. Anderson hooted to her grandson Mervin, who hooted back. It wasn't supposed to be funny, but everybody started laughing. The more Mrs. Anderson and Mervin scowled, the more they looked like owls, and the harder we all laughed. Mrs. Anderson and Mervin finally gave up and plodded off the stage huffing and hooting about how we didn't appreciate good birdcalling when we heard it.

All I had to say was "Mervin," and Grandma Lily would begin to laugh. Oh, how I wanted to hear her laugh again. But she wouldn't even open her eyes. There was no color left in her face. At least the shivering had stopped.

I reached under the blanket to touch her hand. It was cool, not as cold as before, but nowhere near as warm as my own.

I couldn't help wondering if Grandma Lily was going to die. I knew she'd die someday. Everyone does. "But, please, God," I prayed, "don't let her die now. We still need her." I didn't say my prayer out loud, but I know God heard me. That's something Grandma Lily taught me—that God always listens—but He may not answer right away.

The February I turned nine, I prayed for a new bike for my birthday. When I didn't get it, I was angry. Tyler had a bike. So did everyone else in my class. It wasn't fair. I needed a bike, too. "Shucks," Grandma Lily said. "God's not running Bikes"R"Us. Take it from your old Grandma, you'll get that bike someday. The wait will make it even more special."

I got the bike the next May, when the weather was perfect for bike riding. I hopped on my new bike and rode it across the yard to Grandma Lily's. She cheered. "To everything there is a season," she said, "and this is the perfect season for bike riding." She reached out and gave me such a big hug that it nearly knocked me off the bike.

That's the way I always think of Grandma Lily—strong and sure. It was hard to see her so pale and quiet.

I asked God to help us help her. "What should we do?" I said out loud.

I nearly jumped when Rosie answered. "Let's move a mattress in here. She'd be more comfortable on a regular mattress."

Grandma Lily keeps a rollaway bed in her sewing room in case somebody sleeps over. That's the mattress I hauled into the living room. I put it right next to the fireplace. Together, Rosie and I dragged the sled next to the mattress, and as carefully as we could, we lifted her onto it.

"We're getting good at this," Rosie said. We covered Grandma Lily in more quilts and blankets.

"If only she would open her eyes and smile," I said to Rosie. "Grandma Lily has the world's greatest smile."

Right on cue, Rosie began to sing. It was *Annie*, of course, but it wasn't a bad choice. Rosie kept on singing "You're Never Fully Dressed Without a Smile," but Grandma Lily didn't smile. She didn't even open her eyes.

Rosie stopped singing and dancing. She sank forlornly onto the couch. "Something's dreadfully wrong, North. When I sing, the whole world should wake up and listen."

One thing about Rosie: she doesn't have any self-esteem problems. But this time, it was going to take more than one of Rosie's songs to solve our problems.

19

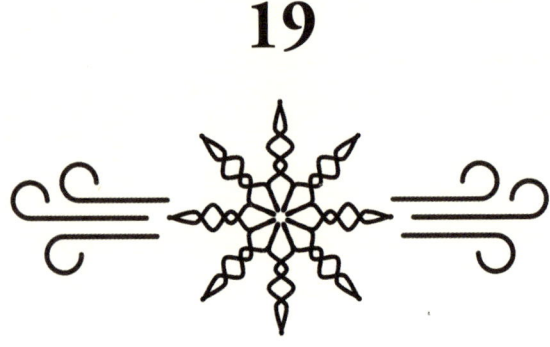

The Radio

I settled in front of the fire and listened to the radio. There was lots of talk about Ada. Some people were calling in from cellular phones reporting on the flooding. I wished we had one of those. That would have solved all our problems. But Dad said they were too expensive. "Wait till they've been around a while. Then the prices will come down." High prices didn't stop other people from buying them.

"We need help out here," one caller said. "Is anyone coming to help us?"

No one knew the answer.

A dad called in. "I need diapers. Anyone know where I can get some diapers for my two-year-old son?"

"Where are you calling from, sir?"

"I'm down here in Breckenridge. I been using towels since yesterday. I'm in dire need. The boy's not slowing down."

I started to laugh.

"What's so funny?" Rosie said.

I told her.

"At least we don't need diapers," I said.

We listened to Jack Sunday warn people against venturing out. "The roads are treacherous," he said. "No travel advised."

Rosie wandered into the kitchen and found some potato chips, cookies, and cans of root beer. She set out a picnic on the floor beside Grandma Lily. Every so often, either Rosie or I reached over and touched Grandma Lily or spoke to her. "You doing okay, Grandma Lily?"

"We love you, Grandma Lily. You're going to be fine."

But Grandma Lily never opened her eyes. She moaned once. I wasn't sure if that was a good sign or not.

When we got hungry, I found the crackers and cheese. Rosie dug around in the pantry and found Grandma Lilly's stash of chocolate chip cookies. We carried them into the living room and munched in front of the fire.

"We never had the marshmallows," Rosie said.

"I forgot."

"I didn't," Rosie said. She found a package in the kitchen.

Outside we use sticks to roast them, but inside? I searched the kitchen drawers and found some long wooden skewers. "These will do."

"Wait!" Rosie said. "I'll get the pickles."

"Pickles?"

"Sweet and sour. Marshmallows and pickles."

It sounded weird to me, but I have to admit, the combination worked. We roasted a marshmallow, ate a pickle, and roasted another marshmallow. Every time Rosie bit into the pickle, she pursed her lips and shook her head, which made me laugh, and she started laughing, too. For a little while, at least, life was as sweet as roasted marshmallows. I forgot that we were in trouble, terrible trouble, and not even sour pickles could spoil the fun.

The hours passed slowly. We listened to the distress calls on the radio. People from all over the Red River Valley called the radio station. Everyone had a story to tell about the rising floodwaters, the lack of electricity, or the raging blizzard. Some people called hoping for news of missing relatives. I wondered if Mom and Dad would call in to the radio station to tell us about the baby. That would be a terrific way to hear the news. But in all the time I listened, they didn't call. Neither did anyone else I knew.

I stared at the fire and lost track of the radio.

"North!" Rosie yelled. "Listen."

"We have reports of at least ten towns and about 60,000 customers without electricity. Northern States Power, the Minnkota Power Cooperative, and Otter Tail Power Company are all working round the clock to restore service. Apparently, there have been several times when a lineman makes a repair only to have a storm whip up and tear it apart."

"Does that mean we're going to be powerless even longer?" Rosie asked.

"Sounds like it," I said. Despite the heat from the fireplace, the temperature in the house was dropping. "I better bring in more wood."

20

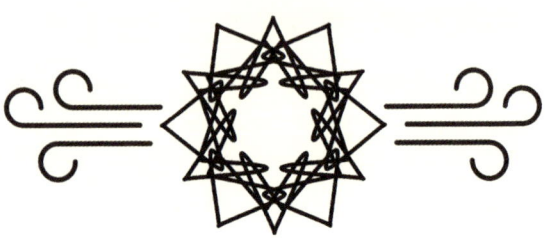

Noah

It took me nearly an hour to gather four more loads of wood. Snow and ice made each trip difficult, but I didn't dare let the woodpile get too low. I wasn't sure how long we'd be without electricity. Because of the water in the basement, I doubted the furnace would work even if the lights came back on.

"No travel advised," Rosie told me when I brought in the last load. "That means Dad won't be home, doesn't it?"

I was tempted to reassure Rosie, but sometimes it is better to know the truth, even when the truth is scary. "I doubt he'll be home today," I said. "We're on our own."

"We're gonna die," she said. "I'm only eight. I don't wanna die."

"It's not that bad," I said. I reached toward her. She slapped my hand away.

"You don't know. You weren't listening."

"To what?" I asked.

"The radio."

"The radio didn't say we were going to die. You're making that up."

"No I'm not. I heard it myself. They said this was a 500-year flood. And you know what happened the last time, don't you?"

I had no idea what she was talking about. "Are you asking what happened 500 years ago?"

"Yes," she sobbed.

"I have no idea," I said. "What happened 500 years ago?"

"Noah."

"Noah?"

"Yes. Noah and the ark. Remember? Only Noah and his wife and his sons lived. Everybody else drowned. Even the animals. He could only take two of each. And he even forgot some of those. That's why there aren't any unicorns or dinosaurs today. I thought you knew."

"I know the story. But what does it have to do with us?" I asked.

"That was a 500-year flood, too. Now it's happening all over again," Rosie said.

"Maybe we should build a boat," I said.

"Stop joking. I'm serious." Rosie buried her head in the sofa pillows. Her shoulders were shaking as she sobbed.

"I want Daddy to come home," she wailed.

So did I. I sat down beside her and pulled her to me the way Dad would have done. "The Great Flood, Noah's flood, was thousands of years ago. Do you remember how the story ends?"

Rosie shook her head.

"With a rainbow. It's the sign that the world will never flood again."

"But our world is flooding right now!" Rosie yelled, and she was right.

"We'll be okay," I said. "We'll find a way to get help. I know we will."

"I don't think so," Rosie said. Tears rolled down her cheeks.

"We will," I said trying to sound as if I believed it. "Remember what Pastor Johnson says at the end of church every single Sunday."

"Sort of."

"He says,

The Lord will keep you from all harm—

he will watch over your life;

the Lord will watch over your coming and going

both now and forevermore."

"Amen," Rosie added, "but …"

"Shh," I said. "Listen."

"—reports that the National Guard is going to begin evacuating stranded residents of Ada."

"The National Guard is coming our way!" I yelled.

"The National Guard is coming," Rosie yelled.

We both jumped up, and we began dancing around the living room. Rosie was still dressed in quilts. We were jumping and hooting, careful not to get too close to Grandma Lily, when I accidentally stepped on one of Rosie's quilts.

She tumbled onto a carpet of crumpled quilts. "North!" she yelled, and then she began to sob.

"Sorry. It was an accident." It really was. There had been times in the past when I've knocked her over on purpose, but not this time. That didn't seem to matter to Rosie.

Her face turned red and blotchy. Her nose began to drip. Her whole body was shaking. There was nothing starlike about her. She wasn't playing a part; she was miserable. These tears were real! I plopped down beside her.

She leaned into me, almost like I was Dad. I pulled the quilts over her and rubbed her back. She's not a bad sister, not really. It's just that she has these annoying moments. Like *Annie*. Like singing and dancing. Like baby talk. Once I got so sick of her talking baby talk to her Weebles that I hid them under my bed. She loved those roly-poly little dolls more than any other toys. I figured she'd fuss, and I'd make her promise to stop talking baby talk, and when she agreed, I'd give them back. No big deal.

But Rosie never said a word about the missing Weebles. She didn't even tell Mom and Dad. She just got real quiet and sat on the sofa for hours staring out the window. When Mom asked her what was wrong, she just sighed.

After a while, I couldn't stand seeing her like that, so after she went to bed, I took the Weebles out from under my bed and put them under hers, where she was sure to find them. But she didn't.

It was Mom who found them when she was sweeping the floor. By then Rosie had joined the cast of *Annie*. She never mentioned the Weebles again. Neither did I.

I knelt down beside her. "I didn't mean to trip you. It was an accident," I said.

"I know," she said. "That's not the problem."

"Then what is?"

"How will the National Guard know we're here?"

I hate it when Rosie makes sense.

21

The National Guard

How would the National Guard know we needed rescuing? "Maybe they'll check from house to house," I said.

"Then we'll be last. They'll check the town first."

"Then we might as well settle in. Why don't you go find some warmer clothes? You can't stay wrapped in that quilt all day."

Rosie bobbled off to Grandma Lily's room, dragging quilts behind her. When she returned, she was wearing two flannel nightgowns over the jeans and T-shirt. Despite her efforts to tie them up with a purple winter scarf, they dragged on the floor. "I got better socks, too," she said, lifting the gowns high enough to show off

Grandma Lily's red woolen skating socks. They reached way past her knees and the heel part was halfway up her calf.

"What do you want to do now?" I asked.

Rosie grabbed a dozen games from Grandma Lily's cupboard, and we settled down to play Sorry! Rosie won three games, and she didn't seem at all sorry about sending me Home. In fact, she was downright gleeful. At least she wasn't whining about being rescued or crying about our likely deaths.

I put more logs on the fire. I love it when the fire blazes and the burning bark crackles, but that day I worried because the pile of logs was shrinking despite my trips to the garage. Grandma Lily must have worried, too. That's why she had gone to the garage. She must have guessed that we'd be stranded for a while, and she was planning to take care of Rosie and me one way or another. Now it was my job to take care of her.

The radio was still on, but the reception was getting worse and worse. "See if you can find any more batteries," I told Rosie. While she went looking, I tried to figure a way to let the National Guard know that we needed help. The phone was out, and we didn't have any kind of two-way radio or cellular phone. There were no lights to flash. Maybe they would see the smoke from the chimney, but that seemed unlikely.

I looked outside. Nothing was moving. If the radio reports were right, there was no way Dad would be returning. Water and ice blocked the roads.

"Look," Rosie said. She held at least ten batteries of various sizes in her hands.

I sorted out the ones that fit the radio and set them aside. "We'd better keep it off. We may need it later." Without the radio, the house was deathly still.

I checked Grandma Lily again. She seemed restless, but her eyes were still shut. She didn't react when I called her name. She felt warmer, but her lips were a ghastly blue-gray. "Sing to her, Rosie," I said. "Maybe it will help." It couldn't hurt.

With Rosie busy, I concentrated on our problem: how to signal the National Guard. I thought about raising some kind of flag, but Grandma Lily didn't have a flagpole. I considered hanging a sheet out the window with a message printed on it, but who would see it?

Rosie jumped up. "Listen. What's that noise?"

I heard it, too, and ran to the window.

"It's overhead," Rosie said. "Helicopters!"

I yanked open the front door and dashed outside. Slushy water reached nearly to the bottom of the top step. Another few inches and the water would be coming into the house. I struggled to see the helicopter, but the clouds blocked it from sight.

"Did they see you, North?" Rosie asked when I closed the door and stepped inside. "Are they going to rescue us? I'd love to ride in a helicopter. Where will they land? How will we get inside?"

I sank down on the couch and stared at the dwindling fire.

"They saw you, didn't they, North?" Rosie looked up at me with such hope that it made my stomach ache. But I couldn't hide the truth from her. She had to know, sooner or later, that we were on our own.

"I don't think they saw me, Rosie."

"Then how will they know we need rescuing?" She cried softly at first and then she got louder and louder until she was wailing. "You promised we'd be okay. You can't break a promise. You have to do something."

And that's when I died a little bit inside. I couldn't do anything. Dad was right. No matter what I tried to do, I failed. I couldn't keep Rosie safe. I couldn't save Grandma Lily. And the last thing I needed was Rosie wailing and screaming. "Shut up, Rosie. Just shut up!"

Brainstorm

I went to the kitchen and picked up the phone. Still nothing. Sleet splattered against the kitchen window, and the air in the kitchen felt damp and cold. It seeped all the way into my heart. I kicked a cabinet. Nothing happened. I kicked it again, and this time I splintered the wooden door.

"North! What are you doing?" Rosie yelled. At least she'd stopped crying.

"Don't come in here." I sank to the floor and began to cry. I wasn't blubbering like Rosie. I don't do that.

But I didn't have enough energy to move. I slumped against the cabinets. I had never felt so useless.

And then something warm slithered against my side.

I yelped. "Rosie! You scared me."

But she just cuddled even closer and said, "It's going to be all right. I know you didn't trip me. Don't cry about it, North."

"I'm not crying. Not about that. It's just that I hurt my toe," I did, too. It was throbbing from kicking the cabinet.

I wiped tears on my sleeve.

Rosie reached over and patted my hand. She picked up a piece of broken cabinet and waved it in front of my face. "If we run out of firewood, we'll burn the cabinets."

That made me smile.

"Besides, you have a plan."

"I do?"

"Of course. You always do." Rosie said.

The tears started again, but I squeezed my eyes shut tight, holding them in. How could she have faith in me when I kept letting her down? "You've been watching too much *Annie*," I said. "Just cause things always turn out okay in the movie doesn't mean they will …"

"I knew you could do it," Rosie said, jumping up and pulling me up with her. "That's a great idea!"

"What idea? What are you talking about?"

"*Annie*. The end of *Annie*. Remember?"

"Sure. Daddy Warbucks adopts Annie, right?"

"Yes. And they have a big party to celebrate. Annie and Daddy Warbucks sing and dance ..." Rosie couldn't resist an opportunity to perform. She began singing.

"Stop," I said as quickly as I could. "What's your point?"

"Well, at the end, after Daddy Warbucks and Annie have danced, the servants write Annie's name on the roof in big lights. So, that's what we need to do. Write a message in big lights on the roof of this house. We could do that, couldn't we, North? I mean, we could use the Christmas lights we brought up from the basement." She smiled and curtseyed as if she were taking a curtain call after the show.

Christmas lights? Maybe. But on the roof? The roof was steep. It was probably slippery, too. I had no idea if I could climb it, and even if I could, there was no electricity.

I shook my head. "I'm afraid it won't work. But we'll think of something."

I wandered back into the living room to check on Grandma Lily. I called her name, but she didn't answer. Dog came over and nuzzled Grandma Lily.

When I plunked down on the couch, Dog jumped up beside me, and we both stared at the fire. Sparks jumped from the logs and fell back into the ashes. It was mesmerizing. "Look, Rosie," I said. "It's really beautiful."

"Sort of like the Fourth of July," she said. "It reminds me of sparklers."

Sparklers? Fireworks. Here I'd been looking for some way to signal the National Guard, and it was sitting right there in our kitchen all the time. Rosie was right. At long last, I had a plan.

23

The Trip Home

I told Rosie that she had to stay with Grandma Lily while I went to the house for supplies. "The Christmas lights?" she asked.

"Wait and see. You keep Grandma Lily warm."

"Maybe you shouldn't go, North. What if you can't make it back? What if you fall in the water?"

"I'll do my best. I have to go. If anything happens, just …" I couldn't think of any useful advice to give her. I'd have to make it. I clenched my teeth. I couldn't fail. Rosie and Grandma Lily were depending on me.

"North?" the voice was weak, but it was Grandma Lily's.

Rosie and I raced into the living room.

"Grandma Lily!"

We knelt down beside her.

"Are you children all right?" she asked, her voice quivering.

"We're fine," I said, "but we've been worried about you. Do you hurt?"

"My hip hurts a bit," she said. "Did I fall?"

"In the garage. You hit your head, too."

She reached up and touched the bandage and then she reached out for me. "You did this? You got me inside?"

"We both did it," Rosie said before I could answer. "We both brought you inside and patched you up."

Grandma Lily closed her eyes, took a deep breath, and sighed. "You children are a wonder. Now, I need to get some rest."

"Not yet," I said. "You should drink something first ..." and before I even finished the sentence, Rosie jumped up and ran to the kitchen. She was back with a full glass of water.

She started to hand it to Grandma Lily, but it spilled as soon as Rosie bent down. "I'll fix it," she said and headed back to the kitchen.

Grandma Lily still held my hand, but her eyes were closing.

"Hurry, Rosie!" I called. She appeared with a glass half-full and a straw. It took both of us to get the glass near to Grandma Lily and to guide the straw into her mouth. She took a sip or two.

"Try a little more." It was important. We gave her the straw, and she took another sip.

I pulled the covers up around her face and leaned over to whisper in her ear. "I'm going to get help. You just rest. I'll be back soon."

Rosie stayed with Grandma Lily while I hunted around in her hall closet for a pair of dry boots. I found her old gardening boots, and while they weren't particularly warm, they were at least dry.

"Maybe you don't need to go now," Rosie said. "She's already getting better."

"She still needs a doctor."

Rosie nodded. She knew I was right.

"I'll be back as quick as I can," I said.

I found some warm socks and a pair of trousers in Grandma Lily's dresser. They were miles too big around the waist, but I tied them over my pants using a belt from one of Grandma Lily's dresses. The pants were lime green, the belt orange paisley, and the boots red rubber. I looked like a demented golfer in a horror movie. When I caught sight of myself in the bedroom mirror, I jumped. I looked ugly, very, very ugly, but I was going for warmth, not style, and with luck no one except Rosie would ever see me dressed like this.

I clomped back into the living room. Rosie laughed when she saw me, but I didn't mind. Laughing was sure better than crying.

"You look awful," Rosie said. "I dare you to go to school looking like that."

"You should talk." She was wearing the red Annie wig and two of Grandma Lily's flannel nightgowns tied with a purple winter scarf.

"I look like an actress."

"More like a big purple pig dropping," I said, and hurried into the kitchen. I put on my jacket, hat, and gloves. They were wet, but better than nothing. Before I left, I tied Dad's emergency rope to the kitchen door. If I tied the other end to our door, it would serve as a safety rope on the way back. I couldn't risk slipping into a puddle with my arms full. I hadn't minded that the doll and pillow had floated away, but I couldn't let our distress signals disappear.

Rosie came to the door. "Be careful, North," she said.

24

Frozen Out

The water at the foot of the steps had turned to ice. Everything was freezing. I pulled on the rope and stepped onto the ice. I sank into icy water. Grandma Lily's gardening boots didn't provide much protection.

Once I had both feet on the ground, snow-covered water swirled around my ankles. I slid one foot forward, then the other, pulling the rope behind me. It was definitely easier to travel the short distance alone in daylight than it had been earlier in the darkness with Rosie and Dog dragging me down.

Once I reached our house, I started up the steps. I slipped on the first step but caught myself before I crashed. The stairs were solid ice. I felt out of control like the first time I climbed onto a skateboard.

At first, my wet boots slipped and slid, and I couldn't seem to get a firm grip. I finally figured out how to ease my feet forward in slow motion one step at a time. As soon as I got close enough, I grabbed the handle of the storm door and looped the rope through. I pulled myself up the last step.

"Made it," I thought, but I spoke too soon. The door wouldn't open. I turned the knob and pulled. Nothing happened.

I tried again. No luck. Was it locked? Frozen?

I tried to remember if I'd locked it when Rosie and I left in the morning. I didn't think so. We never lock the door, and I wouldn't have bothered anyway. Nobody was likely to stop by for a visit, let alone for a robbery. We don't have anything worth stealing.

There was ice all around the doorknob and more ice between the door and the doorframe. It was frozen stuck, and my pounding didn't do any good. My hands were getting colder and colder. They felt numb.

I was about to turn back when I saw Grandma Lily's door open. "What you doing, North?" Rosie called. "Hurry up."

"The door's frozen," I yelled back, hoping she could hear me over the wind. "It's stuck."

"Well, unstick it," she screamed. "I need you."

"Is Grandma Lily okay?" I yelled back.

"She's still sleeping, but I'm getting scared. Come back, North. Please come back."

Sometimes I forget that Rose's five years younger than me. Seeing her standing in the door reminded me that she was just a little kid who needed her big brother's help.

"I'm doing the best I can, Rosie," I called, hoping I sounded strong and confident, 'cause I sure didn't feel it.

How was I going to get the door open? A hammer, maybe, or a knife? "Hey, Rosie. Go to the silverware drawer and toss me a butter knife. I'll chip the ice away."

"We're not supposed to play with knives."

"Rosie! Just get the knife."

She closed the door. A few seconds later, she returned. "I'll throw it to you."

Rosie tossed the knife out the door. It landed about halfway between Grandma Lily's house and ours. It skittered across the ice and disappeared beneath the freezing water.

"Try again," I called.

This time Rosie got a whole handful of butter knives. She threw one, then another, then another. Not a single one landed anywhere near enough for me to grab it.

"You have to try to catch them, North."

"Yah, well, you have to throw them so I can reach them!"

"I can't," and I knew she was right. Then I noticed Dog standing in the open doorway behind her.

Maybe Dog could bring me the knife. I'd seen a movie once, or maybe it was a cartoon, about a dog that brings hot cocoa to freezing mountain climbers. Dog might be old, but he's smarter than any cartoon dog. It would take me too long to make my way back to Grandma Lily's, get the knife, open the door, retrieve the boxes, and then return to Grandma Lily's. I got tired just thinking about it. "Get another knife," I told Rosie, "wrap it in a kitchen towel, and give it to Dog. He can bring it to me."

I sat down on the step to wait.

A minute later Dog lumbered out the door with a kitchen towel in his mouth. I hoped that Rosie had wrapped the knife securely inside.

"Here, boy!" He trotted over to me.

"Good Dog!" I petted him. Sure enough, there was a knife wrapped inside the towel. I chipped away at the ice around the door, and when I yanked really hard, it opened!

I was in.

Dog padded into the house behind me.

Except for the lack of wind against my face, the inside of the house didn't seem much warmer than the outside. I made my way to the pile of boxes on the kitchen floor. Rosie and I must have moved two dozen boxes. Now they were in a jumbled mess. Which one held the answer? I couldn't even remember what it looked like.

I found Christmas decorations, Mom's summer blouses, Dad's family photos, and the papier-mâché turkey Rosie made last Thanksgiving. I found the model airplanes, a box of yarn, plastic containers Mom was saving just in case she needed them.

I didn't find what I needed until I'd opened eight other boxes. They were in a sturdy box at the bottom of a big pile of boxes. I opened it only enough to see the red, white, and blue paper wrappings. I might fail, but at least I'd fail trying.

The rope guide worked great. I held on to the rope with my left hand, clutched the box of fireworks with my right, and started back to Grandma Lily's. Dog led the way.

Whoosh!

He slid down the stairs.

Crack!

He broke through the ice and yelped.

"Dog!"

He whimpered in response. It was the saddest sound I'd ever heard.

I wanted to rush to his side, but my arms were full. I couldn't risk dropping the box in the water.

I worked my way back up the steps, opened the door, and placed the package just inside. Then I scrambled back down the stairs and slid over to where Dog lay in a puddle of slushy snow and icy water.

"You okay, boy?"

Dog lifted his head and whined.

"Can you get up, boy?" He had broken through the same ice that had trapped Rosie earlier.

Dog tried to stand, but he couldn't get a foothold. I noticed a small stream of blood flowing down his left hind leg.

25

Surprises

I grabbed Dog around the stomach, hauled him out of the water, and hugged him tight. He tried to climb inside my jacket as if that would be warmer. He shivered and looked up at me. Ice coated his floppy ears, and he looked at me with big questioning eyes as if to say, "Why did you make me come outside. I'd rather lie by the fire."

It was too late for that. I lowered him onto solid ground.

His legs held him. I sighed. What a relief!

He shook from head to toe, showering me with icy water.

"Can you walk, boy?"

Dog tottered toward the house.

"Stop there!" I yelled.

He did and tilted his head toward me, confusion in his eyes.

"Sorry, boy. I can't risk you taking another fall. Those steps are slick."

I reached out and petted him. "Good Dog. Stay here."

He shook, spraying more icy droplets into the chilly air, before sitting on his haunches.

I climbed the slippery stairs one more time, retrieved the box, and rejoined Dog.

"Come on, boy." We slowly crossed the icy divide between our house and Grandma Lily's.

Rosie greeted me at the door. "What took you so long? I heard another helicopter while you were gone. Did you get the lights? How are you going to climb up on the roof? It might be slippery."

Then she noticed the blood dripping onto the kitchen floor. "What happened to Dog?"

"Cut his leg on the ice." I reached for a dish towel. "Here, boy. Let's get you fixed up." The cut wasn't deep, and once I applied pressure, the bleeding stopped. I wrapped the towel around his leg. Dog played me for sympathy, looking up at me with his big, sad eyes and then nuzzling my armpit. "You can rest now, Dog. Rosie and I have work to do."

I ripped off my too big, too cold boots and retrieved the box I'd hauled home. I handed it to Rosie. "Go on. Open it."

She ripped it open.

"Fireworks!" she yelled. "Sparklers, firecrackers … this is terrific. Are we going to shoot them off? All of them?"

"Whatever it takes," I said.

I could picture a spectacular fireworks show exploding over the house just like in the movie.

"It's illegal, you know," Rosie said. "You don't have a permit. Dad always gets a permit." I hate that know-it-all attitude that Rosie gets.

"Got any other ideas? "I asked.

Rosie didn't answer.

"Well then, we shoot off the firecrackers. I suspect jail's no worse than sitting here in this cold house watching Grandma Lily die."

"North! You know I didn't mean that."

"Good." I wasn't worried about jail. I had a bigger problem to figure out: like how to set off the fireworks without blowing up the house in the process.

Rosie dug into the box of firecrackers. She lifted one item after another out of the box. "Giant Twitter Glitter." She read slowly, sounding out each word. "A large red and green fountain with whistles and a multi …"

She handed it to me. "Multitude," I read.

"Yes. 'Multitude of firecracker reports.' What's that mean, North?"

"It means it's really loud."

"Oh, goody. Look at this one. It says, 'Royal Flush Cone and Carnival Cone. A long-lasting rush of colorful spray.' This is going to be great," Rosie squealed.

"Can I do it?" she asked.

"Do what?"

"Light the fireworks." That was just like Rosie. I do the hard work and she gets the glory.

"Nope. It's too dangerous. Kids should not play with fireworks."

"You're a kid."

"Am not. In two months I'll turn thirteen. I'm almost a teenager. Besides, this is an emergency. I'll be careful."

Rosie looked at me like I was some kind of math problem, and then she said, "I don't think you should do it," she said. She was staring at one of the packages.

"Wait just a minute." My voice was getting shrill. "You wanted me to climb up an icy roof to string lights across it, maybe break my neck in the process, but now you don't want me to set up some fireworks."

"Listen," she said, sounding just like Miss Hannigan. She grabbed a package and began to read: "Warning—shoots flaming balls. Use only under adult super ..."

She handed the package to me.

"Supervision," I read.

"You need an adult," Rosie said. "Dad's not here. Mom's not and Grandma Lily's not really here either." Tears tumbled down her cheeks.

I took the package from her hand. It said *"EXCALIBUR"* in big letters. It was a reloading launcher with six fireworks balls. Actually, she couldn't have chosen a better package. It was one thing Dad had let me help him with last summer. He showed me exactly what to do, and he stayed close while I lit the fuse. Yup. This one would work.

I turned to Rosie. "Here's the deal. I'll just use this one package. It shoots six shells into the air, one at a time. It's really loud—it whistles—and when the balls are high enough, they explode into beautiful colors. Remember?"

Rosie nodded.

Grandma Lily has a small deck at the back of her house with a patch of lawn between the deck and her garden. "I'll use Grandma Lily's lawn," I told Rosie. It's far enough from the house and covered with snow. It's safe, and I'll be very careful."

It wasn't a bad plan. The deck was high enough to be out of the water, and I'd only be in the wet snow for a few minutes at a time. I knew it wouldn't be easy, but it was workable.

"And I wouldn't do it if it wasn't an emergency," I assured Rosie, "but we've got to get help. Right?"

Rosie nodded. "Can I at least watch them go off?" she asked.

"Of course. Just look out the back door." It led to the field behind Grandma Lily's house.

I looked at the package. "*Excalibur*. 6 shots. *Maximum blast*." The directions were below little cartoon pictures of a man setting up the launcher:

1) Set the launcher on a flat surface outside.

2) Unwind the fuse on the fireworks ball.

3) Insert the ball into the launcher.

4) Light fuse.

5) Get away.

I could do that. I'd have to do it six times. That's what we had: six chances to call for help. The rest of the fireworks were ground displays or far too complicated and too dangerous. This was our only chance.

I grabbed my coat and gloves and slipped into an old pair of rubber clogs that Grandma Lily kept by the door to the deck. They wouldn't provide much protection, but I wouldn't be out for long.

26

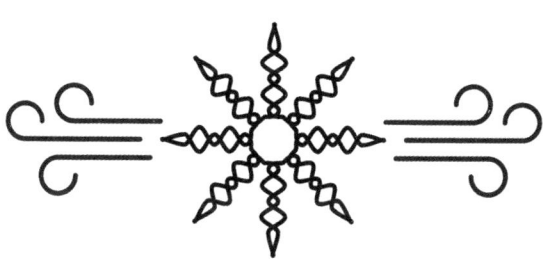

Fireworks

I put some matches in my pocket and carried Excalibur out the door. Drat! I'd need something flat to place beneath the launcher. It took me a while to get a board out of the garage and haul it through the house onto the deck and then down to the lawn. I set the launcher down, unwound the fuse, and put one ball into it. Ready?

I looked at the sky. The clouds had cleared away for the moment, and it had stopped drizzling, but it wasn't dark enough for a fireworks show.

I gathered up my supplies and trudged back to the house.

"What's wrong?" Rosie asked.

"It's not dark yet."

"Oh."

I plunked down on the sofa. The fire was still blazing strong, and we had enough wood to last for a while.

Rosie lay on her side on the floor next to Grandma Lily.

"The fire's beautiful," she said. "I wish Mom and Dad were here to watch it with us."

I'm not sure how long we gazed at the fire, mesmerized by the flickering flames, but the next time I looked outside it was dark enough. Even if the lights didn't attract attention, the noise would.

Rosie murmured something to Grandma Lily. "I told her what we're going to do," Rosie said. "I told her not to be scared."

"Good."

"But I'm scared, North. What if the fireworks set fire to the house?"

"That's silly. Dad taught me how to be careful, and I'm not setting them off anywhere near the house."

Rosie put her hand in mine. We were quiet for a second or two. "Someone will see. I know they will."

I carried Excalibur outside. I dropped the first ball into the launcher and lit the fuse.

Then I dashed inside. Rosie started counting: "one, two, three, four …"

Nothing.

I tipped back my head and opened my arms wide.

"five, six, seven, eight …"

Still nothing. I hung my head and rubbed my neck.

"nine … ten …"

HISS!

The ball shot out of the launcher and sailed into the cold night air.

Rosie's eyes grew wide. She covered her ears as the ungodly shriek continued.

Red and green streamers of light showered down from the sky and color rained on the house: reds and greens and blues and yellows.

"Do it again!" Rosie shouted.

I ran back out, unwound the next fuse, dropped the ball into the launcher, lit it, and ran inside. It burst into the sky, whistling even louder than the first and spraying the sky with colors.

It did it again, and again. Six times in all.

It was terrific. Winter fireworks. For a few minutes at least, I forgot that we were fighting for Grandma Lily's life. I forgot about the baby and Mom and Dad. I forgot that Rosie was depending on me. I simply watched the rainbow of colors arch over the yard, blurring into the fog like the Northern Lights.

"It was amazing," Rosie whispered when the last colors died away.

"Spectacular!" I said. "Stupendous, too."

"Yep, stupendous."

It was astonishing, astounding, dazzling, fantastic, magnificent, sensational, stunning, and wondrous. In fact, Roget himself, the guy who wrote the thesaurus, couldn't have found enough words to adequately describe the glory of our fireworks.

"Is it enough?" I whispered.

Rosie snuggled against my arm. "It's enough," she said. "You're a genius."

"Well, maybe not a genius," I said. I looked at Rosie and laughed. "At least this proves that I know how to blow things up."

After the fireworks were spent, the sky became gray again.

Grandma Lily slept on. I knelt by her side and took her hand. "It's going to be okay," I whispered. "We'll be rescued soon."

Rosie and I sat by the dwindling fire and waited.

But no one came.

"I wish I had my *Annie*. Could I at least turn on the radio?"

"Sure, why not?"

We huddled together and listened. "Water's rising on the Red," the announcer said. "And those folks in Ada are still battling the flooding of the Marsh and Wild Rice Rivers. Here's some interesting news just in. There's a report of fireworks in Ada, a regular pyrotechnic display. The National Guard is on its way to check it out. What do you think of that, folks? Here they are in the middle of the worst flood in Ada history and someone decides to celebrate?"

Rosie looked at me and smiled. "That's us, isn't it, North?"

"It's gotta be, Rosie. Celebrating, huh?" I gave her a friendly bump on the shoulder.

"Hooray! Hooray! Hooray!" Rosie yelled.

The National Guard would find us within an hour. We set up the fireworks around eight o'clock. They'd be here by nine.

Nine came and went.

Then ten.

Rosie yawned. "Aren't they coming?" she asked.

"They'll be here," I said with more confidence than I felt. "Maybe it's too dark now. They'll come in the morning." I crossed my fingers for luck.

"You mean we have to wait another night?" Rosie wailed.

27

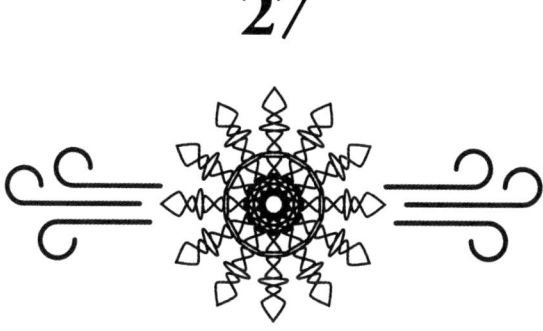

Confession

"I don't know, Rosie." I shrugged and walked to the bedroom to grab a load of blankets. "We might as well sleep here in the living room with Grandma Lily."

"Near the fire?" Rosie asked.

I nodded.

Rosie gathered more snacks from the kitchen while I built up the fire. We ate crackers and cheese, and then Rosie found a package of Oreos in the cupboard. We finished them off, too.

We tried to play Chutes and Ladders, but Rosie kept hopping up to check for the National Guard.

"They won't be here until morning," I said after about the fifth time she ran to the window.

"But I want them to come now," she said.

I stoked up the fire. The house got chilly the further we moved away from the fireplace. "Maybe you should get some more blankets."

Rosie marched off to Grandma Lily's spare bedroom and came back with two more blankets. "We'll be toasty warm," she said. I made up a bed for her on the floor next to Grandma Lily and one for me on the sofa.

"You're the best brother in the world," Rosie said as I tucked her in.

"Not really," I said.

"Oh, but you are," Rosie said, and her kindness hit me like a punch in the stomach.

I sighed and thought of all the times I'd been unkind, like when I made a big fuss about going to see the community theater production of *Annie*. Dad thought Rosie was too young to audition, but she begged to do it. "I may be small, but I'm not young!" she argued. Dad gave in. For days she practiced singing and dancing along with the movie. She memorized the dialogue. By the time auditions began, Rosie knew every single part by heart. Still does, of course.

Mom and Dad made me sit through at least fifteen rehearsals and all six performances. Oh, I complained all right, but Dad didn't give in. "You'll go to support your sister."

Rosie didn't need or want my support, but that didn't matter to Dad. The entire audience followed every tap of her shoes and each tilt of her head. She didn't miss a beat—or a line.

"Adorable," the old ladies said.

"Precious," said Mom's friends.

"A terrific new talent in the role of Molly," read the review in the *Norman County Index*, our local paper. Mom framed the article. Rosie memorized that, too.

Darla saw the show. So did Ty. And they both said Rosie was terrific. But I never told Rosie that. I should have because, truth is, she was, and I was proud of her.

And there was the time I stole her Weebles. It felt like the right time to confess.

"Rosie," I said, "Remember when you lost your Weebles?"

"Sure. I loved those little people."

"Well ..." I took a deep breath. Why tell her? Maybe she was better not knowing, but before I could say anything, she said, "You took them."

I squeezed my eyes shut. It was better if I didn't look at her. "I'm sorry," I mumbled. "It was wrong, but I gave them back, didn't I?"

"Not soon enough. I looked everywhere. I even took the stepladder from the kitchen and looked on the top shelf of your closet—"

"Rosie! That's private. You had no business …"

Rosie sidled away and hung her head. "But they weren't there, and when I couldn't find them, I took something of yours."

"You're the one who took the farm? How could you?" I glared at her and cracked my knuckles. "You took it outside."

"I pretended it was a dollhouse. I made the cutest little stick people for it, and I hid it beneath the bushes. I thought maybe fairies would come and live there. And then I forgot. It's still there, North. I'll get it back for you."

"No! It's not there. It fell to pieces. How could you do such a thing? That model was important."

"So were my Weebles. But you took them, and you hid them. I was just treating you the way you treated me. That's the Golden Rule: treat others the way they treat you."

"No way. You've got it wrong. 'Do to others what you would have them do to you.' It means that you should treat others the way you would like them to treat you. You switched it around. You turned it into revenge."

"Revenge? I don't get that. What's revenge?"

"It's what you did—taking my model because I took your Weebles. It was wrong, Rosie."

"But you took my Weebles."

"That was wrong, too. But two wrongs don't make a right." It's something Grandma Lily says. I'd never really understood it before.

"I'm sorry about the fairy house," Rosie said. "I'll make you a new one."

"You can't. Dad gave me it to ME. I was supposed to pass it along to my son." I collapsed onto the couch. I couldn't even look at Rosie.

She plunked down beside me.

I pushed her away.

Rosie reached over and rubbed my arm. "We should forgive each other and start over. I won't touch your things ever again."

But it was too late. The farmhouse was ruined. I could never fix it. All this time I'd been feeling bad about the Weebles, and Rosie had done worse. I couldn't do a thing about it, and now we were stuck together in a cold house that was getting colder.

"Go to bed," I barked.

"But I'm not tired," Rosie said.

"Then stay up. Stay up all night if you want."

I checked on Grandma Lily, and then I plunked down on the couch.

I was nearly asleep when Grandma Lily stirred. "North," she murmured.

"I'm right here." I jumped up, fully awake. "How are you feeling?"

"I've a bit of a headache," she said. "Maybe you could help me up. I've got some aspirin in the medicine cabinet."

"I'll get them for you."

Rosie popped up and knelt beside Grandma Lily.

"Keep her company while I get the aspirin," I said.

Rosie told Grandma Lily about the fireworks while I grabbed the aspirin and a glass of water.

I put two aspirins in Grandma Lily's hand and held the straw up to her mouth.

"That's good," she said. "I was thirsty."

"Have some more."

She sipped a bit more, and then pushed the glass away. "That's better. I should get up and fix you children some supper."

"We already ate," Rosie said. I tried to get Grandma Lily to drink some more, but she refused.

"Would you like me to sing to you?" Rosie asked, and she didn't wait for an answer. It was a lullaby that Mom sang to us—one that Grandma Lily had sung to her:

> *Sleep, my child, and peace attend thee*
> *All through the night.*

28

Rescue

I woke up once during the night. The fire was dwindling, so I added a few more logs. I didn't wake again until Rosie nudged my shoulder.

"They've come! The National Guard has come to get us!"

A tall man in an army camouflage jacket was waiting by the door. He looked stern. A tag was sewn onto his jacket pocket: Lt. Erickson. "You kids responsible for the fireworks?"

"Yah," I said.

Rosie moved as close to me as she could get. I didn't push her away, either. "Don't arrest us," she said. "We just wanted to get your attention."

"I don't plan to arrest anyone, little lady. If you wanted attention, you've got it."

"You're not mad?" Rosie asked.

The big man smiled. "Do I look mad?" he asked.

"Well …"

And then he smiled.

"No!" Rosie shouted. She put both arms around the man's waist and gave him a giant hug. "Come meet Grandma Lily," she said, taking his hand in hers and leading him into the living room. Other soldiers followed, all wearing green camouflage gear and white rubber boots.

"You sure you won't arrest North?" Rosie asked Lt. Erickson.

"North?"

"My brother. He's the one that shot off the fireworks."

"No. There won't be any arrests. Now let's get you kids and grandma out of here."

A medic was checking Grandma Lily. Other soldiers carried a stretcher into the house and carefully lifted Grandma Lily onto it. They carried her outside and lifted her into their truck. The flooded road had turned to ice, big chunks of it. No wonder they brought a heavy-duty truck.

"You two are next," one of the soldiers said. He wrapped Rosie in a heavy blanket and carried her outside.

"I don't need any help," I said, quickly, so that no one would try to carry me away. I rushed into the kitchen to get Dog.

"Sorry, kid," the soldier said. "People come first. Cats and dogs come second."

"But we can't leave him here. He'll die."

The soldier paused, but then he started shaking his head. "Nope. Can't do it, much as I'd like to. I'm real sorry about that. People are our priority. We've got to get your grandmother to the hospital."

I held my ground. I couldn't leave Dog. He'd starve on his own. What would happen when he needed to go out?

"How about this? I'll call animal rescue. They take care of pets. Now, I'm not promising anything, but it's the best we can do. Come on. Your grandmother and sister need you."

I didn't say goodbye to Dog. I couldn't. It was all I could do to walk out that door and climb into the truck. I didn't look back. If I did, I knew I'd lose it. It was bad enough my Dad thought I was a loser. I couldn't cry in front of the entire National Guard. I just couldn't. So I stared out the back of the truck as we drove through the watery streets of Ada.

Waves lapped up onto the houses in town. No one said a word as we passed the Dekko Center, Ada High School, and ARC Lanes. All the buildings were encased in ice. I wondered about the books in the library. Were they frozen? Do books thaw? And what happened to the bowling alley? Would Ty and I ever go bowling again?

A helicopter waited for us in the road just past the Cenex station. It rested on hard-packed ice and snow. Soldiers helped us climb inside.

"This bird will fly you to the hospital. Your folks are waiting," the pilot said.

29

Reunion

The helicopter was smaller than I expected. And it was noisy. After one of the National Guardsmen strapped me in, a medic took Grandma Lily's pulse and asked me her name and age. I yelled to him above the noise. Grandma Lily's stretcher filled up almost the entire space. Rosie covered her ears against the loud whirring of the copter.

I sat next to the window and stretched my neck to a sky that was filled with clouds. Whenever there was a clear spot, water stretched for miles across the land. The river was all but gone. It had become a lake.

She pulled at my jacket as the helicopter started to land.

"Where are we?" she asked.

"The hospital."

"Mom and Dad's hospital?"

"Yes," I said. "You've been here before."

We'd come to the Fargo hospital with Mom during one of her checkups. She had taken us past the nursery so we could see the new babies.

"This time we'll get to see our baby."

Doctors and nurses met us on the hospital roof and carried Grandma Lily inside. Rosie and I stood out of the way.

When the rush of stretcher people passed, a nurse signaled us to follow her. "There's someone inside who's eager to see you," she said.

"Dad!"

We both ran into his outstretched arms. He hugged us tight; I squirmed free. "You're suffocating me," I said.

Dad led us down a hall to Mom's room.

She was sitting in bed holding a small blue bundle in her arms. "A brother," she said. Her smile felt like a hug.

I nearly laughed with relief. A brother.

"A brother?" Rosie said. "But I was hoping for a girl."

"We don't always get what we want," Dad said. "Brothers aren't so bad."

When I looked up, Dad smiled at me.

Rosie crept closer and closer to Mom's little bundle.

Mom laid the baby on the bed and pulled back the blanket.

"We've named him Storm Warning," she said.

"Storm Warning?" Rosie asked.

"Storm Warning?" I asked.

"Yes," Dad said. "Your mother wanted to name him Robert, after me, but I want my children to be one of a kind. We decided to name him for the weather. After all, we spent most of the time we were waiting for him watching the nightly storm warnings. "It was between Flood and Storm. We opted for Storm. He's the only Storm Warning Olson in the entire world."

Poor thing, I said to myself. But it could have been worse. Flood? Floody. Stormy seemed a little bit better. Maybe he'd grow up to be a meteorologist.

I looked at the baby. He had a huge head at the end of a bird-skinny neck. Scrawny little legs poked out from his oversized diaper. His face was cherry red except for a few white pimples on his cheeks. His hair, what hair he had, was so white that it looked pink against his red skin. When he breathed, the top of his head puffed in and out, as if he was some sort of river waiting to flood.

"He's so tiny," Rosie said.

"Not as tiny as you were," Dad says. "He's a healthy 8-pounder with the lungs of a lion." Dad smiled at me, then. "I worried about this little one," he confessed. "I feared he'd be too tiny, like you, Rosie, or have lung problems, like you, North, but he's perfect."

Not like us, I thought, but Dad must have been reading my mind. "You two turned out perfect, too," he said. "I don't think you kids have ever seen a newborn baby up close."

I hadn't. I bent down real close, and just when I started to pull back, the baby opened his eyes. They were bluer than a summer sky, and when he looked at me, his eyes locked on mine. Little as he was, he reached right out and grabbed my finger. His skin was so soft that I feared it would tear. But he was stronger than he looked. He didn't let go. He held me tight and pulled my hand toward his face. Then he opened his mouth wide and cried. Mom reached down, covered him up, and lifted him into her arms.

I plunked down in the metal hospital chair. "Storm Warning," I said. I had to love a brother named Storm.

After all, the kid seemed to like me, and if there was one thing I knew for sure, a baby named Storm was going to need a big brother.

30

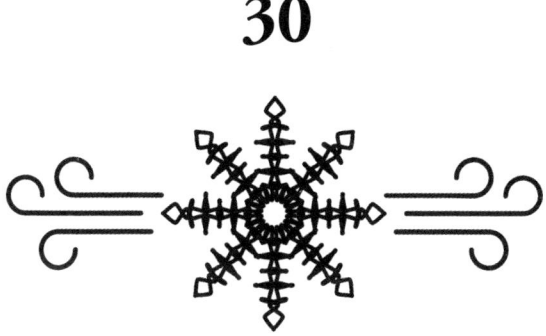

Tomorrow

Rosie and I told Mom and Dad everything that had happened. They weren't upset even when I told them that the basement was flooded and that the water had reached the first floor. "We're so thankful you kids are all right," Mom said.

Last of all, I told them about Dog. My voice cracked when I said, "I left him. He's all alone in the house."

"I forgot all about Dog." Rosie wiped at her eyes.

Mom reached out to her, but not Dad. He looked directly at me.

I put my head down, shifted from foot to foot, knowing that whatever he would say couldn't make me feel any worse than I already did.

He cleared his throat, moved closer, and put his arm on my shoulder. "It was a lousy choice you had to make, North. But you did what you had to do."

That was all—I stumbled back and let out a deep breath—but it was enough.

A doctor popped in with the news that Grandma Lily was going to be all right. She had a broken hip and a concussion. "She was lucky that the children found her and warmed her up," the doctor said. "I expect she'll make a full recovery. It will take some time and therapy, but she'll be fine."

"She's a fighter," Mom said.

"There is a roomful of reporters waiting downstairs to speak with the young heroes. Are you willing to give them an interview? They heard the calls over the National Guard radio, and they want the full story."

"A roomful?" Mom asked.

The doctor nodded. "We have reporters from the *Fargo Forum* and a TV crew from WDAY, PBS, and other local stations. We expected that. But we've got news crews from all over the country, too. You might just make the national news."

I gulped. National news? "Do we have to?" I asked Dad at the same exact moment that Rosie said, "Let's go," and grabbed Dad's hand. He motioned for me to follow. It wasn't a choice.

The doctor led us to the hospital conference room. A National Guard spokesperson was already there. She had begun telling the story of our rescue. "Here they are now," she said as we entered the room.

They made room for us in front of the microphones. The doctor stepped up and gave a brief report on Grandma Lily's condition. He also mentioned that we had a new baby brother. "Any questions?" he asked.

"That must have been quite an adventure," a reporter said.

Dad pushed me forward. "Uh, yah," I said softly.

"What was it like watching the flood getting closer and closer?"

"Um …" I opened my mouth, but nothing came out. It was as if my mouth and brain were no longer connected. I sputtered for a few seconds. All of a sudden, Rosie jumped in front of me.

"It was terrible," she screamed into the microphone. "We were freezing and even though we got a fire going, it was still cold." She pointed to her fuzzy socks as if to prove it. "I tried to make Grandma Lily smile," she flashed them her toothiest smile, "but nothing worked. I sang to her, I covered her with warm quilts, I tried everything, but she just wouldn't wake up." She sighed and shook her head.

I couldn't believe it—Rosie had taken over. She looked ridiculous wearing her silly red *Annie* wig and those huge flannel nightgowns, but she smiled like a TV star. The reporters loved her!

I slipped into the shadows and watched the Rosie Olson show.

She told them everything in her own way.

"I knew we had to get help, but the phones didn't work, so we couldn't even call 911. The TV didn't work, either, but that reminded me of my favorite movie, *Annie*." She smiled her biggest *Annie* smile, and then she put up her hands and said, "Fireworks!"

Several reporters clapped.

"What are you going to do next?" one asked. "I don't suppose you can go home for a while?"

"No," Rosie said barely stopping to catch her breath. "We've had some hard knocks, what with the flood and all, but there's always …" She stopped speaking for just a second, looked at the microphone in her hand, looked into the cameras and said, "There's always … tomorrow …" and then she burst into song, *Annie*'s song.

The television and radio people recorded the whole event. The newspaper reporters took photos. And when Rosie stopped singing, everyone broke into applause. Some even cheered.

Rosie beamed.

When Mom walked in with baby Storm, the reporters took pictures of Rosie looking lovingly at Storm and Mom. Suddenly, Rosie looked up and spotted me in the shadows. "North," she called out. "Get over here!"

I turned away and ran smack into my Dad. "Rosie's a little … a little …"

"… pig dropping?" Dad said, putting one of his huge hands on each of my shoulders.

31

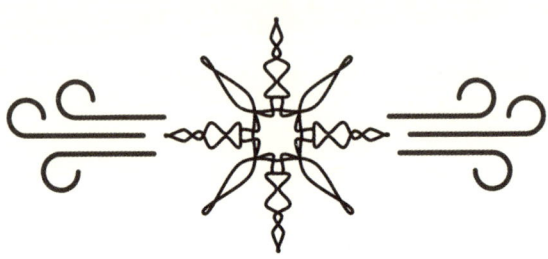

A Hero's Tale

He pulled me toward him so that our faces were only inches apart. "It's what you wanted to say, isn't it?"

That or something worse. But I didn't say a thing.

"Rosie's Rosie," Dad said. "Always on stage, always the star. She's not like you, North. You're a—"

And I waited, seeing the word *loser* appear in an imaginary cartoon bubble above Dad's head.

"—you're a hero," Dad said.

I blinked and my throat got tight. My voice broke when I tried to speak. "Not a real hero. Not like you."

Dad's voice turned harsh. "You mean because of this?" He yanked up his sleeve so that I could see that jagged white scar.

I nodded.

"That's all in your head, North, and it's about time you heard the truth."

He led me over to a plastic couch and pulled me down next to him. "We were in the desert. My unit—we were mechanical—kept the jeeps running. Winds whipped up. It happened all the time. Sandstorms. I'd never seen anything like it. Imagine this winter's blizzards with sand instead of snow."

He paused, and I nodded for him to go on.

"So, one day I was working on an engine, trying to get it to quit stalling, when the wind picked up. Next thing I knew, blood was pouring out of my arm. Not a bomb. Not a bullet. Nothing heroic. Just some piece of scrap metal carried on the wind. It slit my arm from wrist to shoulder. Took the doc two hours to clean out the sand and stitch it up. So there's your war story. I'm no hero. I was just a soldier putting in his time, doing the job I was given."

"But I …"

"I know what you thought, but I've told you the whole truth. I was afraid you'd think less of me if you heard the real story. But now you know. I was simply a soldier doing his best at a difficult time. Like you," he said, drawing me close and squeezing me against his chest.

That's when I started to cry. "Sorry," I sniffled, wiping my sleeve across my eyes. I was sorry that he got hurt, sorry that I'd pestered him about the scar, sorry that I was the kind of son who cried like a baby when he was sorry.

Dad put his hand on my shoulder. "Don't worry about it," he said. "It's the relief, that's all. The battle's finally over. The flood was as vicious as any enemy, and you faced it with courage. You brought your sister and your great-grandmother safely through the storm. I couldn't have asked for more."

When I glanced up at him, it was like looking out a wet windshield. "Guess I'm tired," I said.

"That, too," Dad said. "You've heard Mom say that you were sick when you were born. Your lungs weren't fully developed. We nearly lost you. I never shed a tear when the doctor told us how slim your chances were. Your mom did, but not me. I was the strong one. But on the day they finally let me hold you, the day they said you'd grow up to be strong and healthy. That's the day I cried."

I wiped my eyes on my sleeve. Dad kept his grip tight on my shoulder. "We better see what Rosie's up to now," he said as we started walking back toward the cafeteria.

"I've been hard on you this winter," Dad said. "Maybe I was worried that this new baby would run into trouble. Your mom's getting older, and if it happened once, it could happen again. That and the flood and some problems at work."

"Problems?" I asked.

"Resolved," he said. "Everything is back to normal. But when it was happening, I took it out on you. I didn't mean to, but it made me hard to get along with."

"Like Rosie?" I said, and we both began to laugh.

"Yah. Grown-ups can get cranky, too. But that's over. Your mom's fine. The baby's fine, and I know that he'll grow up to be as strong and clever as his big brother."

"And his Dad," I said. It's not so bad being the son of a hero. Sometimes it rubs off.

32

After

Later that night, we watched the TV news in Mom's hospital room before we went to the Super 8 to get some rest. I was exhausted, but Dad said he was sure we'd want to see the news since we might be on it.

Rosie was terrific. They showed her entire interview, including her song, and the anchorwoman had tears in her eyes by the end. "What a little trooper. Someday we'll all be hearing big things about Wild Rose Olson."

Rosie was much quieter than usual. "Anything wrong, Rosie? You were wonderful," Mom said. "And we're all together now. That's what really matters."

"It's North," she said.

"North! I hoped that maybe you two would have learned to get along."

"Oh, we have," Rosie said quickly. "It's just that ... well, North was the real hero, but maybe it didn't sound like that on the news. I didn't mean to leave you out, North. It's just that, well, once I had the microphone in my hand and the lights on my face, well ... I ..."

She looked sorry, and she looked like she meant it. "Yeah," I said. "I understand." And I did. Rosie is Rosie. She's a star. Me, I just want to be left alone to find my own direction.

We were about to leave when a nurse popped in with a message. She handed Dad a pink note.

"It's for you," Dad said. He passed it to me.

Attention: North Olson

From: Lt. Erickson

Of: National Guard

Message: Dog safe at Dr. Lyle Hummel's. Doc says he'll board the dog until you can pick him up.

"Dog's safe!" I tossed the note in the air.

Rosie cheered, Storm cried, and Dad grabbed me and gave me a bear hug.

"See. Everything turned out all right. Now let's get you two to bed."

When we woke up the next day, John Wheeler, our weatherman, was calling our storm the eighth blizzard of the winter. Folks in Ada called it a "fluzzard." After all, we had both a flood and a blizzard at the same time. Dad said we wouldn't be able to go home for a while, so we tried to make the motel room feel like home. Five people crowded into a room with two double beds get cramped quickly. We made do.

We didn't make it home for another two weeks. We picked up Dog on the way. He climbed onto my lap and licked my face the whole way home. Dog doesn't hold grudges.

The water had receded. Grass was growing, and Mom's flowers were popping up around the yard.

"What are those shiny things on the lawn," Mom said.

Rosie started to giggle. So did I.

"What?" Mom asked. "What are they?"

"Grandma Lily's butter knives," I said.

"And how did they get on the driveway?" Dad asked.

This time I told them the story.

"It may be years before we hear everything that happened," Dad said, and he shook his head, poked me on the shoulder, and said, "It was quite the adventure, wasn't it?"

"A once-in-a-lifetime adventure," I said.

"Let's hope so."

Of course, the flood did its damage. The washer and dryer, the furnace, and the water heater were a total loss. Dad and I hauled everything that was left in the basement to the street. There were piles of debris everywhere. The town planned to haul it away.

We spent all spring cleaning up from the flood. We were luckier than lots of folks. We didn't lose any furniture, and Rosie and I had saved most of the valuables from the basement.

Grandma Lily spent a few weeks in the hospital. She still walks with a limp, but she's baking again and the polka music blasts from her kitchen window just like it used to. One day when I was helping her with her garden, she said, "I wish I could give you a medal for saving my life, North, but I know you wouldn't want one."

She was right. What would I do with a medal? Besides, there were too many heroes for medals. Practically everyone helped with either the sandbagging before the flood, the rescues during it, or the cleanup after. We did what needed to be done, which was what Dad had done in Kuwait.

Thanks to that news conference, Rosie's face was on the front page of the *Fargo Forum*. She even made newspapers as far away as Chicago and New York. She was smiling beneath the curly red wig and the caption read, "Brave little flood victim proclaims that 'the sun will come out tomorrow.'" Clips of Rosie singing played on all the evening news programs, and pictures were in the weekly news magazines.

"I'm famous!" she yelled when she saw the paper. "I should be in the movies."

"Yah, right," I said, which made Dad scowl.

"Sorry," I whispered, and he nodded.

"Fame is fine," Mom said. "But it doesn't last." She gave Rosie a hug. "I think being a regular kid is a lot more fun."

"Like North?" Rosie said.

"Yes," Mom said. "North knows what really matters. Right, North?"

I was holding Storm at the time. "Family," I said and winked at Storm. He started to giggle, and Mom swooped us both into a big hug.

Stormy is a great little guy. When he sees me, he giggles and raises his arms so that I'll lift him out of the crib. I can already tell that we're going to be great friends.

Maybe years from now, Storm and I will work together on a sandbag line. Maybe then I'll tell him all about the Great Flood of 1997, when he was born and we were saved by the National Guard. I'll have to be careful, though, because I wouldn't want him to feel guilty for taking Mom and Dad away on that stormy April afternoon. After all, everything turned out all right in the end. And if another flood comes our way, we'll deal with it together. No problem. Right? Right!

THE END

Author's Note

North and his family are not real; they are fictional. So are his friends and teachers. However, a dangerous flood did occur in the Red River Valley of the North in the spring of 1997. The Red River begins where the Bois de Sioux River and the Otter Tail River come together near the twin cities of Wahpeton, North Dakota, and Breckinridge, Minnesota. The Red flows north and forms the border between North Dakota and Minnesota. It ends at Lake Winnipeg in Manitoba, Canada. Like the scar on North's father's arm, the Red River twists and turns for a total of 545 miles, although the actual straight-line distance from beginning to end is only 315 miles.

In the winter of 1996–1997, a record amount of snow fell in the Red River Valley. By March, 110 inches of snow had fallen. It didn't begin to melt until late spring. Volunteers began filling sandbags and building dikes when National Weather Service meteorologists predicted floods.

Winter was officially over when the last blizzard hit. It began with an inch and a half of rain on Saturday, April 5. Later, it turned into freezing rain. Power lines fell, covered with ice. By Sunday, April 6, rain turned to snow. Total snowfall for the year measured 117 inches, and floodwaters filled the towns along the river.

The city of Ada, Minnesota, was particularly hard-hit. Volunteers used half a million sandbags to keep floodwaters out from the city. But the dikes weren't enough. When the April blizzard hit with 70-mile-an-hour winds, the water from melting snow overflowed the riverbanks, turning farmland and city streets into lakes. The floodwaters froze, making roads impassable. The National Guard rescued many of Ada's 1,700 residents and closed off the city. The people of Ada weren't allowed to return home for days. In Ada, the flood and blizzard became known as a "fluzzard."

How to Help When Floods Hit

If you live in an area that is likely to flood, listen to the weather reports. If the National Weather Service advises you to evacuate or leave the area, tell an adult. It's important to follow the advice of the experts. Sometimes there will be plenty of notice. Other times, floods happen quickly, and the best thing you can do is to leave and go to higher ground.

If your community has advance notice and is preparing for a flood, you may be able to help fill sandbags or build dikes. You may be able to help your team, club, or church prepare or deliver food to those who are building dikes. After the flood, you may be able to help with cleanup.

If you want to help people after a flood or other natural disaster, donate money to an organization, like the Red Cross, to help them rebuild. You might organize a school fundraiser or work with a church or other community organization. Ask an adult to help you with this project.

About the Author

Elizabeth Raum has written over 150 books for young readers, often choosing to write about places she has lived. During the 1997 floods in the Red River Valley, she was living in Fargo, North Dakota. As she watched elementary and high school students fill sandbags and build dikes, she wondered what would happen to kids who were home alone as floodwaters rose. North, Rosie, and Grandma Lily are fictional characters who stepped up to provide a possible answer. To learn more about the author, visit her website: www.elizabethraumbooks.com.